FOOD BOWL

GIL HARDWICK

Published by **eNovella Australia**, Perth, Western Australia

Typesetting, Layout and Cover Design by **Site211 Media**

This edition printed and bound by *https://www.createspace.com/*

National Library of Australia Cataloguing-in-Publication entry:

Author: Hardwick, Gil.

Title: Food Bowl / Gil Hardwick.

ISBN: 978-09923704-3-5 (paperback)

Target Audience: For young adults.

Subjects: Science fiction, Young adult fiction.

Dewey Number: A823.4

Inspiration

Inspiration for this book is partly life experience; partly Doris Pilkington Garimara's *Rabbit Proof Fence*, Xavier Herbert's *Poor Fellow My Country* and Frank Herbert's (no relation) *Dune*; partly Jim Leslie's *The Mal'lam Voyagers*, and partly of course Ayn Rand's *Atlas Shrugged*. Against climate change and global warming, queer politics and the current parlous state of Western democracy, the remainder is entirely speculative.

Contents

PART THREE

PART FOUR

PART ONE

Chapter One

From their lookout high up on the lip of the scarp they could see the light haze billowing up from the distant headers as they churned their way across the waving yellow-brown rice paddy, drift easterly on the mid-morning sea breeze. The Doctor, they called it.

The blokes taking the crop off would be happy. All week had been dead calm and the fine stuff coming off the great wide contoured paddocks had hung around on the still air; finding its way into their eyes and ears, right up their nose and down their throat, if they weren't wearing their suits and respirators.

It wasn't only the fine clay dust off the ground getting inside their clothing; working its way into their pores, into their armpits and crotch, but old pollen and itching plant fibre coming out of the headers themselves, and off the dry straw churning out onto the new stubble behind them as they passed over it, and again as the winnowed grain came pouring out of the auger tube into the tractor bin trailing alongside. Ten tonne to the hectare they were getting.

But now there was other dust; fine light plumes from vehicles approaching, this time through the thick tree cover down to their right. There looked to be three of them close together, with a fourth bringing up the rear some distance behind.

Mike turned his spotter's scope onto them, and picking up their GPS radioed in their location before his mate tapped his arm. Swivelling his scope around, he spotted another convoy coming in from the northwest at 10:50 o'clock, but still some distance away.

With his first radio alert the boys on the ground moved quickly into position, spreading out into the tree cover well out from the edge of the crop; covering the men on tractors while others around the air-lift field bins checked their ammunition and clicked their rifles off safety.

The headers were a good way out and fairly safe across a kilometre or more of flat open stubble, and they were due to shift the field bins closer to them anyway. These ferals arriving here on the northern boundary right at this moment only meant their timing was off; assuming they were after trouble or had some strategy in mind, or something had simply held them up; it was well past smoko, almost lunch already.

Within minutes the deep thrumming clatter of gunships coming in low above them, hovering, covering their flanks, drowned everything else out. Behind them came the steadier roar of the big transporters moving into position ready to drop their refills and take the full bins off.

Finally Mike ducked behind some rocks away from the noise, and covering his ears yelled into the microphone for his men to hold the perimeter and keep them there; take the refill bins out closer to where the headers were working then come back and take the full ones off - be quick about it - make sure the harvested grain was secure and he'd be down shortly to see what the newcomers wanted.

And tell the tractor drivers to stop out there where they are, or better turn around and go back out to the headers; we'll drop the empty bins near them so they don't have to come any closer.

Something was up and it bothered him. Where the ferals should have been was miles away at the silos where the company maintained a beggar's gate, where they knew they could pick up rations and take them away in their small jerry-built trailer bins filled with third-grade grain, or seconds occasionally, depending on the season.

Coming here in so many vehicles must be costing them a huge fuel ration, unless they had a digester or a still hidden away somewhere, and plenty of fuel grain from past years to feed it.

Whatever it was could only mean trouble.

The crowd was milling about quietly by the time he made his way down the long slope onto the flat and through the trees, leaving his mate up on top as lookout.

There was another lot over to his left that the men kept under guard, but right in front of him was fairly peaceful, non-threatening. Glancing across the boundary fence into the stubble he saw that his orders had been carried out, and only two of the gunships sat watchfully at rest there on the ground where the bins had been while harvesting went on a good safe distance behind them.

They were all waiting for him, turning to look at him as he strode purposefully from under the tree cover.

Straight away he recognised their leader, and he called out to him.

"Ed, what the fuck? You know better than this . . . fucking bullshit. You know the rules, we have an agreement."

Chapter Two

"Mike, talk to me!"

He gazed back down the corridor. Peter Jamieson had his head stuck out his door, looking in his direction. Casting his eyes down a moment, hand on the doorknob, he cocked his head and glanced back again.

"Got something?" he wanted to know, knowing very well that the company boffin did have something important to say else he wouldn't be calling him; "Give me 10-15 minutes, OK?"

Placed his briefcase wearily on the sideboard along one wall, he opened it taking out a thick sheaf of papers. He stepped across to the desk to see a pair of red and green lights flashing in the top corner of the glass tablet set before his chair. The green indicated a security definition update so he flicked his finger across the screen to enable it, while the red told him there was a board meeting at 1300 hours and he was expected to attend with a full report.

It was not yet mid-morning, however. Outside the sunlight angled across the city, its rays muted by traffic haze even on the sunny side of the tall buildings, apart from the bright flash off some window somewhere. He stood, gazing thoughtfully out across the city skyline, then turned and stepped across to his ensuite for a quick shower and freshen-up.

His shoulder and hip were aching. As he dried himself off he stopped to check the pock marks and scarring up his left side; souvenirs of that little stoush on the Horn of Africa when some guy had sprayed him with a 9 mm Uzi from an empty building across the town square. It was that come-down off the adrenalin rush of action that did it to him every time, and he thought for a moment maybe he should go see a psych finally.

Shrugging it off, he dried himself with a clean towel and looked at himself in the mirror. His body was still clean and fit, well-muscled without an ounce of fat. His pecs and abs, and as he turned around his shoulder blades and dorsals, were all well-toned with clear definition beneath thick dark body hair. Back at boarding school, even as a teenager they called him The Bear, from his father's side who were all swarthy Mediterranean types; Black Irish they called them, except he'd been a swimmer and now sported well-developed shoulders and upper chest with slim waist and hips. He had a quick shave before putting on clean briefs and a t-shirt, then dressed again in his bush uniform. More or less presentable he went out into the tiny kitchenette to grind fresh coffee beans, and wait patiently for his miserly allocation of water to boil.

He smiled ruefully, thinking about it. No matter how much it rained - and during the monsoon it bucketed down - all the water was allowed to runoff regardless, and here they were with their tea or coffee allocation carefully metered by the centralised mainframes. Water.com had their niche in the scheme of things; no doubt of it, but so did Energy.com for more substantial reason. It was their windmills and solar panels, after all, which covered every roof as far as the eye could see. For all they were concerned rain came down from the sky for no better purpose than to wash the dust off their equipment.

The coffee was exquisite; Pitalito Estate *Caturra Supremo*, shipped in from the southern Huila region of the Colombian Northern Andes in South America. The job did come with its perquisites, but he was good at it. He had a reputation for bringing crops in on time and under budget, with a minimum of conflict, and had personally trained an awful lot of the world's top sowing and harvest managers. Most of the time he simply handed his ordinance back unused at the end of the season, he was that good, and was issued with entirely new gear as needed at the start of each job. They looked after him.

The raw sugar he preferred came in from the Monymusk factory, off the Caribbean south coast of Jamaica. He liked their bigger bean, No. 1 Blue Mountain coffee as well; they'd send it packed in his regular sugar order with no questions asked, but he relished the fruit, sharp acidity and slightly bitter after-palate of the Pitalito.

He could have his sweetener brought in from Beenleigh in Queensland if he wanted, or Coffs Harbour, but with world fossil fuel reserves so badly depleted the super-fast wind-powered neo-clippers that now dominated world commerce tending easterly in these latitudes with the trade winds, it was cheaper to ship produce from the Caribbean, Brazil and Argentina to the Australian west coast than just about anywhere else on earth. From here they'd take their grain shipments on the roaring southern latitudes back with them. It hadn't taken anything for the old colonial sea lanes to reopen, he thought, except these days real luxury came in unannounced as back load tucked in under the empty grain compartments.

Snapping out of his thoughts, he turned to pick up his cup. He was tired, bone weary after months of stripping canola, wheat and barley, then rice, right through spring and the hot summer months and looking for a break between early sowing and late, which was about the only time he had to himself. Thinking again he put the cup back down and placing some fresh beans and sugar in sachets put them in his pocket. Taking up his cup again he went out into the corridor, along a few doors to find Peter's office wide open, waiting for him.

The guy was Autistic; Asperger's, or so somebody said. Hyperactive brain, incredible mental acuity. Food.com had him on the payroll too for good reason.

"Shut the door?" he wanted to know, but the other simply waved him in.

"No, don't worry, they'll be right. Something to show you. Come and look."

Peter was leaning over a huge, round, slightly convex glass screen set into an enormous desk. Looking down into it gave a sense of vertigo, as if looking down through clear sky onto the planet from some orbiting geostationary spacecraft, the image was so clear. The thing was his own invention, dating back to his internship with the old Food and Agriculture Department while he was still at university, still a kid really, when somebody there taught him GIS mapping and he was seriously hooked.

He had a mate over at iVEX who let him use up spare CPU time on their latest 56-node quad-core iVEX-B supercomputer, so long as he downloaded his data in real time and stored them locally here in the Food.com building, down in the basement where he'd installed the old 28-node iVEX-A. Somehow or other he had networked the two engines, updating the old operating system in line with the new iVEX-B, so while iVEX gazed up at the stars through their Tanami Widefield Array, their satellite relays allowed Peter Jamieson to gaze knowingly back down on the planet.

"Yep, what have you got?"

Peter flicked his fingers across the screen as if it were an oversized Android tablet displaying a gigantic, three-dimensional, super high definition Google Earth. He spun the globe about so it oriented true north from where Mike stood, then pushing the ground away from him zoomed in on the southeast of the greater metropolitan area.

He and Mike had known each other for nearly 30 years. He'd been providing him with high level intelligence for over 20. There was always a minimum of words between them; good minds at work. Mike simply followed his direction, focussing on the ground unfolding beneath him.

Peter was a master at it. The experience of looking down into the thing was like hang-gliding above the city, orienting himself to the huge perimeter wall, and the great steel grid gates and barriers over rivers and streams where they rushed down off the scarp across the old prehistoric sandy flood-plain.

"There!" Mike said suddenly, "Come about."

Peter traced his right forefinger in a gentle arc, respecting potential updrafts and wind currents - the man is an artist - bringing Mike back to where he wanted to be but now a mere 20 virtual metres above the top of the southeast wall.

There was a small child on the track, half under a tree, but outside the wall not inside where he should have been. Mike glanced back as he flew over, and right on cue Peter flicked him back to see a woman rush out and with an anxious look up at the sky drag the boy back out of sight.

Before he left he slipped him his sachets of sweet caffeinated bliss knowing he'd be hyper for two days and functionally useless to all and sundry, but pleased as punch nonetheless.

Chapter Three

"Come out, you know who we are."

"No, mate. We know what you are, but who are ya, right?"

Mike turned back to his signalman, and on his nod called again, "Bede, mate, come out and stop fucking me around. You know it's me, and you know I don't bullshit with anyone."

"It's not Bede. He's not here."

"Who is it, then? Charlie? Frank?"

"Norman."

"Mike . . . Barker. You know that, Norman. Who have you got with you, mate?"

"Just us, wife and kids."

"Where's Bede?"

"Ah, mate, don't start asking me shit questions. It's right, all right?"

Chapter Four

The rock concert on the Oak Lawn was in full swing, with gaggles of adolescent girls and the occasional spotty undernourished youth standing there amid the packed crowd, trembling and swaying on the threshold of physical pain before the huge speakers; blasted into ecstasy by the 120 decibel sound system and whatever else they were on. Only the helicopter gunships coming in to attack were that loud, intending to subdue their target through sheer clattering din before firing on them if need be.

Mike shrugged and walked around the other way, behind the Law Library, and entered the Social Science building via the back stairs. Clambering up three flights he pressed the button to open the automatic fire door then made his way down long narrow corridors until he reached an obscure little office overlooking the Oak Lawn that looked as if it might be a cleaning closet, and knocked on the door.

It opened shortly to reveal a squat though otherwise unremarkable professor in shirt sleeves and bow tie, shaking his head in real annoyance. Sound hammered at the windows, the air heavy with it as if compressed into the small space somehow, making the room with its piles of books and papers seem much smaller than it already was, claustrophobically so.

The other said nothing for a long moment, then taking Mike's arm closed the door behind him and led him back along the long corridor and down one flight of stairs, until emerging again from the stair well he went along a few doors and opening one entered a large empty conference room. Pulling a couple of chairs out he sat in one and indicated to Mike to do likewise.

As he did so he rose again, muttering apologies for being so rude and asking whether Mike would like tea, or coffee perhaps? Glass of water?

As Mike declined with a wave of his hand he sat again.

"Well, Mike, it's been a terribly long time, old chap. To what do I owe this honour?"

"Professor Harding," he said slowly, "you carried out doctoral research years ago on city wall security. I've read your thesis. I want to know more about on what basis you made your estimates and predictions."

"By God, what? That was 40 years ago. I went to Milan after that, then Paris, and Madrid. My dear fellow, there is no comparison with Europe. The idea of a secure walled city with protected agricultural lands here in the Antipodes in those terms is silly. It was silly then and it's silly now; quite the reverse of conventional wisdom, though with the late machine age and robotics I can see the logic. I made a point of making my views heard on the matter. This wall of ours doesn't even compare with the Israeli West Bank barrier, or Johannesburg which has no great city wall of course but walled housing compounds nonetheless. What I mean to say to you is, town walls traditionally keep others out so as to protect the citizens from attack, not to keep people in so as to protect agriculture, even from overpopulation."

"Ha!" he interrupted himself, before Mike could speak, "As a defence our wall would fall at the least protest; it's so badly situated."

Mike watched him a moment, waiting, and when it was clear the professor was ruminating; eyes gazing thoughtfully now into a distance, took the chance to speak.

"Yes, I understand that. What I want to know is more about the foundations, and how they came to be undermined so badly by the weather."

The other gazed oddly at him for a moment, then declared, "Well, they were designed to keep people in, not out. The reinforcements run along the inner wall, not the outer. There was nothing to stop water rushing down off the scarp after a winter storm from washing out the gravel beds on that side, and over time holes simply appeared in the ground inside the wall, lifting tarmac off the perimeter road, and lawns in parks. In engineering terms, old chap, it's no different at all from building a gully dam and expecting it to hold, precisely so."

"Anyway, my thesis as you know, if you have read it, is not about engineering but on such a device as a failed social experiment. Already children were crawling out through the holes over summer, to play in the bush. They were building cubbies in the holes at first, then began to crawl out further until they found themselves outside the wall itself. Nobody acted at the time because it was only children playing. The wall itself was considered a sufficient psychological barrier to serve its intended purpose, with positive conditioning as you can see within the city itself to keep the people mindless and happy, so nobody did anything."

"My thesis was shelved, you know. Too close to the American thing, that long fence along the Mexican border, and they didn't like it one bit."

He paused a moment and gazed off again into the distance, then sighed and shrugged before turning back to him. "I've only been back 2-3 years, as a Winslow Professor on half-pay, and my little office of course," he said finally. "What's been happening, Mike, tell me."

"The simple fact is, Professor, most of those kids in your time are now grandparents. Their children and now their grandchildren are still going out, except through holes beneath the wall big enough to drive a small truck through. That's what's been happening."

"And what would you like me to do about it? What can I do for you?"

"Not a lot, I guess. I wanted to know your thoughts on the matter, and whether you knew of anyone else working in this area who might be able to advise us. Some of them have gone as far out as the Grain Belt, and want part of the action it seems. There will be a war if we don't act."

Professor Harding leaned forward earnestly. "Melanie Denning, old chaps. She'll fit the bill; very clever young gel, serious pussy and frighteningly sober. Doing her thesis on edge dynamics, you know. Give me your card, will you, and I'll pass it on to her."

Chapter Five

"So, in a nutshell, Mike, what you're saying is the city can no longer contain the people. The walls are ruptured, and people are coming and going to suit themselves."

"Well, Stan, I wouldn't quite say ruptured. It hasn't been breached in the normal sense. It has simply aged beyond redundancy and leaks like a sieve. And it's mostly kids going out through the holes and gaps to play. Older kids are venturing further out, going for long bushwalks, and sleeping out I guess you could say. Those already young adults have become more adventurous, wanting to see the world, grow their own food, experience life. That's the way I'd put it."

"You wouldn't call them criminals, or suspected organised crime, terrorists; political radicals, behind these security breaches?"

"No. I wouldn't think that of them at all. It's negligence on the part of City.com as far as I'm concerned. They've been warned time and again that only parts of the scarp are hard granite; the rest is compacted pea gravel; stratified podsol, especially in the gullies, and over the long period a lot of it has just naturally washed out."

"So, why wasn't it noticed?"

"Because those shits over there have their heads up their collective arse, that's why. They all think if you're up high enough you can see everything, but not one of them ever goes down to street level, out into the perimeter suburbs, to see what real life is like for real people."

"No need to be rude, Mike," the chairman butted in. "We'll have a bit of order, if that's OK with you."

"It's true nonetheless, Charles. How better would you express it? City.com is in contractual breach in their failure to keep the city safe; none of the upper level domains will dispute that, or side with them. The situation has exceeded critical mass, that's why it's hitting the fan right now. The issue of most concern to us is we can no longer guarantee crop security. For this lot of kids coming and going is normal; they don't see anything wrong with it. If we don't do something quick, next season we'll be using live ammo against them."

He sat back, taking a deep breath. He glanced around the board table, then leaned forward again and said deliberately, "If we don't act quickly it will be on our shoulders. Somehow we have to bring matters to their attention, have them accept responsibility for their own wall, and for keeping the population entertained. While we're doing it we'll have to rebuild our field apparatus, our entire operation. The traditional way we've been operating just won't do any more, not with that many stray people wandering about. Gentlemen, it's gone too far, become far too dangerous."

The chairman nodded. "All right," he said finally. "I won't call for a motion, or take it to a vote. I agree, this is a crisis. We'll go around the table, and let's all speak our minds."

He glanced slightly sideways to his left. "Not picking on you, Stan, knowing you're closer to City.com than any of us. You just happen to be sitting there. We'll start with you and go around clockwise, fair enough?"

"No problem. I agree with Mike, but for different reasons. I manage their festival catering, you all know that, so I can see what they're about. Their engineers have been saying the same thing too, quietly. They've been bringing a lot of young blood in, a lot of them from Arts.com and Sex.com, but they haven't been practical about it. The queers don't have a clue, really, and I'm not being sexist in any sense; it's simply the fact of the matter."

"So, what do you recommend?"

"A taskforce, Mike in the lead; I'll put a motion to that effect, but I'm happy to go around the table first. Let's see what else comes up."

Chapter Six

The phone was ringing, and at once a loud banging at the front door woke him from exhausted slumber. He reached over and picked up his watch from the bedside table, its tiny hands glowing fluorescent in the dark telling him it was still only 11:30.

Ignoring the phone after a quick glance he got up and slipping on a pair of shorts went to the door to see what all the banging was about. Opening it he saw a tall slip of a girl standing there, phone to her ear, who squinted up at him in some surprise. She flicked the phone off and put it in her pocket, and the phone inside stopped ringing.

Mike glanced inside then back at her, raising an eyebrow in askance.

"Um, yes," she said sheepishly, "you're Mike Barker, right? Right place, first go, not bad eh?"

She slipped past him and threw her bag onto the lounge, then looking about eventually turned to him. He closed the door, absently snibbing the lock.

"Yes, well, um, Melanie, ah, Denning you know. Art Harding sent me. Sorry I'm late, just got back. Can I stay here, is that OK? I'll get my stuff from Mum's in the morning."

She stood there victoriously, grinning from ear to ear.

"Mike Barker, and me, eh? Now there's a team. We'll piss on those fucks."

She picked up her bag again and going through to the bedroom threw it on the bed, and then stripping off her clothes went straight into the bathroom and turned on the shower.

"Yeah, Mike, like I said, sorry I'm late, and like, I'm really grubby. We can go over to Mum's later tomorrow if you want, once we've got better acquainted, or early if you like then just get started."

She tested the water then stepped into the shower, drowning out her voice, while Mike simply shrugged and went to get her a clean towel. As she showered he made up the settee in the lounge for her, and folding her soiled clothing and taking her bag placed them on the coffee table next to it.

Eventually she turned off the water, still talking animatedly to him as if he hadn't missed a single word, not a beat, except when she came out still drying herself she noticed the made-up settee and her bag and clothes there, and turned to him frowning.

"Ah, what, um, don't you like me already? I'm really nice, it's not a problem. We can keep our relationship separate, and still do the job. I'm very good you know. I thought, like, if we're going to be working so closely, better to get, um, you know, acquainted first. Is that OK?"

"I mean, it's sudden, maybe. We don't have to fuck straight away, if that's what worries you, but we can still sleep together."

"What the fuck," she went on, her voice rising. "I don't sleep on fucking lounges I sleep in a bed, like, what is this shit?"

Mike stood there a moment, gazing absently out the big picture window and across the night skyline, until shaking his head wearily simply glanced at her and shrugged.

"Melanie, OK, right now I'm thoroughly exhausted. I haven't stopped for months, and with all this blowing up suddenly I'm just too tired right now to give a shit either way. So if you'll excuse me I'm going back to bed. You do what you want."

19

When he woke again next morning the sun was just up, the early morning glow softly lighting his apartment. Melanie was in his bed still sound asleep, but across from him with only her arm stretched toward him, her left hand nearly touching him as if she'd reached for him during the night.

He lay there on his side, propping himself up on one elbow to study her. She was taut and trim with no fat and clear muscle tone on her silken skin and lithe, evenly tanned body; lying there even in sleep like an Asiatic cat almost ready to pounce, like one of those Bengali hybrids but without the dappled fur, quietly napping in wait rather than sleeping. But she also had that soft little girl look about her, as if butter wouldn't melt in her mouth.

Eventually he rose and went into the kitchen, not bothering with his shorts this time, and pottering about made scrambled eggs and bacon on toast, decorated with slivers of spring onion with sliced grape tomatoes, two chilled glasses of freshly squeezed orange juice, and two short blacks of his special Pitalito *Caturra Supremo*.

She was there beside him suddenly, nose twitching and eyes flashing in askance, then without a word cast about for cutlery and finding some went out through the glass door onto the balcony and set the small table there. Her exquisite synchrony caused him to smile after her.

Chapter Seven

By mid-afternoon they were back over the wall, not virtually this time from Peter's office but in Mike's personal helicopter, a small, side loading European Neo-Aérospatiale-Tuareg Fennec; a converted international military scout model to his own specification with plush leather seats, but stripped down nonetheless for functionality in place of comfort, or entertaining clients. He just liked the feel of them on a long trip, in an interior more like a passenger car than an aircraft.

It was painted a mottled desert sandy-green with his Green Crop logo on either side, with Benz-Eurocopter noise-cancelling blades bent at the outer end like a kestrel's wings that cut out the thrumming air-chop of conventional blades. Coming in low it was barely observable, quiet, sounding like a routine light passenger plane throttled back as it came in to land; deliberately so as not to intimidate Outback people, and they'd come out happily in their battered old trucks to the landing strip to meet him.

They appreciated his recognition of their abiding fears, and the courtesy and respect he paid them. His reputation had been well-earned.

Over the scarp he turned to Melanie, one eyebrow raised.

"Um, yes, where you had that bit of trouble at your last rice crop, like, where you ran into Bede," she said quietly, "just there will do. They'll meet us there."

Mike leaned forward to instruct Archie, his personal pilot, and the stubby aircraft leaned over slightly south-easterly and set a new course. They arrived in a bit over an hour and set down in the low-cut stubble just inside the fence.

Twenty minutes later two vehicles arrived and they disembarked, leaving the pilot to lift off again once they're unloaded their swags and overnight gear, with instructions to pick them up at the same time tomorrow.

Melanie swung her gear over her shoulder like an old hand, and it didn't go unnoticed. The others paid little attention; there on their own business, but Mike did, and he tucked it away in the back of his mind. Quickly they shook hands all around and as the light 'copter lifted with not much more than a humming whistle they went across to the vehicles and clambered aboard.

Gazing about, firstly at the people then at Bede and back at Melanie, he was struck by their uniformity, not in dress but ethnicity and character; almost as if they were the one big family, or clan or tribe maybe. Sitting back thinking about it, the realisation struck him like a blow, after all these years, that they hadn't quite aced him but had patiently and quietly played more than the odd queen and king over his jacks.

At that moment Melanie suddenly glanced across at him, smiling shyly, then Bede turned around to gaze more directly at him for a long moment across the back of the front seat before turning back again to murmur a few words to the driver. Nobody said anything after that. After a few miles the small convoy merely started to run slightly uphill and disappeared more or less beneath a closer tree canopy.

As the slope steepened and the tree line passed behind them, massed horsemen emerged and gathered about the two vehicles. Quickly, after their presence registered, as suddenly their lines parted and young people on ponies broke through, and after them children, then women, until finally the ranks broke altogether and old women first and then old men stood before them.

Mike sat back impassive. So this is it.

This tribe of beautiful people were all uniformly tall, slim and graceful; the young adults around 180 cm in height; all with sleek honey-brown skin that shone with good health, dark almond eyes and dark brown to black hair, and it sounded silly to think it, all with separated ear lobes many with studs and small jewels that flashed and glistened in the sunlight, that caused him to look more closely. All the dominant human genes inherited in the mix.

Some of them in their facial features threw back a little to Aboriginal, some to the Oriental, and some again to the Caucasian, though for the most part you had to look closely to see any clear differences among them. And there were not just a few dozen, there were hundreds of them.

Melanie stood there smiling at him.

"OK," she said after a long moment, "um, phone your pilot and tell him not to worry about picking you up tomorrow, you'll ride back with us. Then hand your phone in, and anything else they can track you with - you'll get them back - and we'll show you around, eh?"

Chapter Eight

The horses they were riding appeared to have a fair bit of brumby in them, though finer in the head with deep round chests and well-muscled hind-quarters, enormously agile and intelligent, sure footed up in the breakaways and fast down on the flat. They had plenty of stamina.

The boys and girls alike rode them almost without reins, merely touching their flank with either heel if they wanted them to turn, speaking softly as they did so, while their horse's ears flicked slightly listening to them. The horses went unshod and their gear was basic; knotted leather bridle with plaited leather or hemp rope for reins, and most of them on a folded blanket or bare back.

All of them were flash, well-dressed in clean clothes that were obviously well cared-for, and their long flowing hair was neatly trimmed with the occasional beading for decorative effect.

They rode on through the early part of the morning while it was still cool. Last night's briefing was short and to the point, people speaking little, and when they did they spoke cleanly and well with clear phrasing and fine economy of words. These were people who didn't say much in the company of strangers, it seemed, not because they were hiding anything but because they didn't have to or find any need to, but the message was clear enough.

The reason they hadn't been noticed as a people for so many years was partly because nobody was looking for them, or paying much attention to them. But in larger part they were clever, and drew little attention to themselves anyway. This large gathering it turned out was for his benefit, for the day or two he was with them before they all dispersed again back among the population; up along the myriad tracks and roads toward the great north-westerly escarpment that separated the huge metropolis on the sandy coastal plain, cut off on the other side by the ocean.

Their evening meal had been astonishingly varied and plentiful; nothing at all he'd expected having only ever known Ed Caston's silo scavengers perpetually camped along the railway lines, accepting God's Portion and their meagre gleanings with it in return for keeping a nominal peace around the district, and living basically on porridge and a few tough vegetables, with the odd bit of meat when they could get it. The rest of their grain ration went into biofuel digesters for their vehicles, where these people here were horsemen as it turned out and kept only a few patched jalopies for their occasional public appearance, leaving an impression they were also scraping to survive and battling for resources like everyone else, apart from the corporate big shots in their city towers who nobody ever saw much anyway.

This journey he'd embarked on with them was to show him around, as Melanie said, but in effect showing off; demonstrating their extent and their prowess, and how much of the country they controlled. They were riding the bounds, every so often stopping to mark a tree or rock afresh, some of the boys dismounting to stand pissing there amid raucous joking laughter until it was the girls turn and they lifted their skirts and stood pissing like the young men, until as their day wore on they conspicuously started forming into discrete groups that rode slightly separated from one another.

Mike began to guess that it was not all entirely for him, but part of an annual event to which he'd surreptitiously been invited. As he glanced nonchalantly across at Melanie riding with him, her sheepish look and slight smile, and the way her eyes flashed, seemed to confirm the fact. It was as much a mass courting as a boundary riding, and the anthropologist in him started taking short mental notes as they rode along.

This was rough country, desiccated for most of the year, covered with low trees and prickly grey-green understorey. Every leaf they met was tough, leathery and fringed with spines. Granite boulders along the ridge tops were coated with pale green lichens and mosses that crumbled like old paint on rotten weatherboards as they brushed past. The ground between was ancient red pea gravel, nodules of exposed bauxite and aluminium ore with occasional sandy patches on the low points, and every now and again a green spot indicating a nutrient sink where odd bits of organic matter puddled when it rained. The riders were oblivious to the hardship as if born to it, ignoring the prickles and cuts and scratches; their horses sure-footed even on the rocky outcrops.

They skirted the railway lines down on the flat, and the tall silos dotted along it like knots in a long rope, except every now and then they came across a group of hobbling silo people and they stopped in among the trees, below the line of the hill if there was one there, or behind it until the outriders gave the all-clear, waiting and watching silently as they passed by.

Around what he reckoned to be lunch time a boy rode up beside him, about 12 or 13 by the look of him, and passed food across; sticky rice with pork and vegetables in leaves, and wheat-flour buns and fresh fruit, and clean drinking water from a plastic goonie skin. The food was delicious, but Melanie looked darkly at him then glanced down at the boy.

"He's mine, Ajani. Hand's off."

Then to Mike, "He's my cousin. Tell him to bugger off. He's going through, like, his gay-boy pre-puberty thing, you know, and he's got the hots for you."

"Third cousin, ah, once removed," Ajani reply curtly. "But we're all cousins so it's not an argument. And anyway he needs a retainer he doesn't have anybody, and he has accepted my food, so you can butt out of my puberty it's not your business, OK? Find your own cock, eh? And just shut up if you have nothing sensible to say."

Mike noticed a few more than Melanie and Ajani now riding with him, with a number of the younger boys with Ajani and quite a few more older boys and girls with Melanie.

He pulled his horse up and they all stopped and turned, watching him.

"Don't I have any say in this?"

Ajani stepped his horse back toward him a few paces and said quietly, "Um, well, no you don't. None of us has, really, it's just the way things are decided among us."

"What happens if I want to be with Melanie?"

"You can, if that's what you want, but you can have me with you too, for when she's working, and anyway my name is Ajani which means I'll win whatever you say, so I wouldn't worry about it too much."

Another boy said quietly, "Yes, you're lucky. Be happy."

He looked around the group, from face to face, to find them all generally smiling at him until eventually Melanie nodded slightly and sighed, then spurred her horse forward and with a slight backward glance in his direction made him ride beside her. Ajani settled in slightly behind, to his right flank, grinning broadly, at which a few of the left-over boys paired up and the rest simply rode on ahead likewise in twos and threes.

For the rest of the afternoon they rode quietly, more solemnly, soberly, taking their duties more conscientiously now with the formed-up groups making their formal observances at each boundary tree or rock more orderly and proper, though with not much less hilarity.

Toward evening as they all rode back into the main camp, the older people were lined up along either side of them, watching them come in and noting seriously who was riding with whom.

Chapter Nine

The assembled gathering that evening was relatively rowdy for a people habitually quiet and unobtrusive. Good food went around with soft murmuring interrupted by chuckling laughter and small groups coming and going. Posted sentries out on the perimeter were relieved on a regular basis, so nobody missed out on the fun.

Melanie sat prominently at Mike's left hand, while Ajani sat slightly back at his right. Nobody failed to notice the arrangement, some chuckling briefly to themselves as they passed by while others nodded wisely. Bede especially came to stand finally before them, smiling as he cast his eye over the party, then leaned forward to scruff Ajani's hair before disappearing again into the glooming behind the firelight.

Mike turned to him slightly, asking, "What was that about?"

"Ah, he's my Dad, so it's OK. He likes me, unna, but he thinks I'm too clever so he checks on me all the time."

"Bede's your Dad? Bede Caplin? So you're Ajani Caplin. Which one are you?"

"I'm like, second, eh? My older brother's Norman, you met him inside the wall a few days ago. Those kids of his are my niece and nephew."

"So, which one is your mother? Who is she?"

He looked up abruptly, staring at him for a long moment before glancing away.

"She died," Melanie said softly, "when he was born. She was a Tan. He was raised by Tempi's family, that's why he and Tempi are so close. They are both the same age, only a week between them, so they were raised as twins."

He turned to her. "Is that right? What else do I need to know?"

"Well, Caplins and Dennings don't get along very well. It's OK, not nasty, like, just different mob. Ajani doesn't quite trust me, is all."

"And, like," she went on, voiced lowered, "maybe you like to boy-fuck too, you know, just covering our bases. I don't mind really, but, like, they can get a life finally."

"Shut up, Melanie. Christ you can talk shit. Just because you got into university and you're doing your PhD, I'll beat you at that too, I'll get a General Exhibition and then I'll get 1st Class Honours; I'm already doing better than you did in Year 10, and I'm still only Year 9."

Mike sighed, and sat back a little so he had both of them in his line of sight. "All right, I get the picture."

He glanced appraisingly from one to the other, and smiled. He looked about him and saw that in every group they were quietly bickering at one another, poking sharp sticks at each other, and grinning as they did so as if it were a game they played. These people are very, very competitive, he thought to himself, boasting proudly the instant one became one-up on somebody else while everyone else around took note of how cleverly they did it. Their fun had an edge to it.

The reason they were habitually taciturn was only partly for safety, he quickly realised, but because every word to them is sacred, immanent with power, and they took care what rolled off their tongue. It was like they were all still children having never grown up, with no grasp what it means to grow up, to detach themselves and think in the abstract; still immersed in that random, spontaneous energy and magical spell of childhood that they had to protect themselves from as much as enjoy.

Every sentence was a magic spell, especially for the younger ones, and as he looked further he saw they all had wards of some sort against them, or sat close to an older person who could fend off the banter and answer for them.

He turned back to Ajani, thinking.

"So, who gave you the name Ajani? Where did you get that from?"

"He gave it to himself," Melanie butted in. "His real name is Gerald."

"No, it's not! Bitch. I'll get you for that. My name is proper and legal, everyone agreed. We had big bijnitch, and it's all proper. You're just jealous, trying to put me down all the time, telling everyone I'm gay."

"But you are. You and Tempi, we all know. Tempi and Ajani are synonymous with Gay."

"You don't know anything. Girls don't know anything about boys. He's my friend that's all. He's my best friend, or was; my second best friend now, unna."

Mike realised he was going to have to get used to all this.

"Who's your best friend, then? If that other boy used to be your best friend and now he's your second best friend, who's your best friend? That other nice-looking boy, riding with you and speaking up for you, that's him, isn't it. Tempi, is that his name? So who's your best friend?"

Ajani looked up abruptly at him, searching his face, gazing deeply into his eyes, his own soft doe-eyes glistening in the firelight. He trembled slightly. "He is, and you are," he said simply. "If I let Melanie just take you I'd be dead, and she knows it. That's why she's being so horrible right now; why she's being such a bitch."

"No I'm not, you little shit."

"All right, both of you, stop it right now. You'll be driving me nuts carrying on like that. If you want to know, I'm smarter than both of you combined. If you make me unhappy I guarantee you'll be sad. When you're sad your soul gets sick and shrivels up, and you die."

He turned to them, speaking quietly now. "The reason you're all so beautiful is you're not sad people, and you know how to be happy. You can make me happy; more happy, unna. So make up, eh, and make up your minds how things are to be or I'll get up and walk away from the lot of you."

"No you won't, you can't," Ajani said, almost under his breath.

"Watch me," Mike said, then abruptly changed the subject.

"What's on tomorrow, more riding?"

The two glanced at each other until Melanie nodded slightly, and relaxed.

"Um, yes, sort of," Ajani said. "We'll ride back north west. Everyone's going home, this is only a day, you know. We'll tell you when we get there, like, where your pilot can pick us up, OK? You can have your phone and other stuff back when we get there, so he can find you straight away."

Chapter Ten

Their mounted escort waited patiently, unobtrusively, back in under the forest canopy while the four of them waited in their town clothes out in the clearing. There were four of them because Tempi insisted on coming with Ajani, and Melanie took his side arguing three's a crowd.

All Mike could think was, these childlike people are so very clever. They'd tested him, probed him to the core of his soul, and after three more days riding with them he thought he was smart but they had him around their little finger; each one of them separately and taking it in turns he had no doubt but with the three of them in concert it was a done thing.

And Tempi was a Tan, not a Denning or a Caplin, from the other tribal division; the third phratry. There were only the three, not two or four as he'd usually expect, not because of their genealogies but because of the way the landscape and its specialisations against the background hostility and neglect of the ruling elites decided how they were to organise themselves. Ajani and his quiet, delicately featured soul-mate Tempi are not gay boys, they are hostage to one another and had been since birth. Now they'd made him hostage, attached to him, sucked him right in. It all made sense.

His thoughts were interrupted by the crackling voice in his ear, and the low humming whistle of the helicopter coming in over the tree tops to hover a moment inquisitively, then settle on the grass nearby like a great fat dragonfly.

The pilot having stowed and secured their gear strapped himself quickly back into his seat, anxious to be off this unknown patch of turf. Melanie had Mike promptly seated next to him in the front, while the three of them clambered into the plush back seat and strapped themselves in to sit tense and unsmiling; faces pale and eyes wide, mouths open in a half grin, expectant, like kids at the top of a roller coaster waiting for the car to fall.

Mike turned to inspect their belts, half-rotating his co-pilot's seat for access, and leaning sideways adjusted their straps and inspected the buckles; speaking softly to them as he did so, until satisfied he rotated his seat and locked it back into place and nodded to his pilot.

Twenty minutes later they were on the helipad on top of his apartment building.

PART TWO

Chapter Eleven

"Gentlemen, I'd like to introduce you all to Dr Melanie Denning. We have as you know just returned from our field survey with information you'll finding interesting, to say the least. With no further ado I'll hand you over to her."

Melanie stood, looking obliquely at Mike as he sat, then around the board table until finally addressing the chair she explained, "With respect, I don't have my doctorate yet . . . I'm not Dr Denning just plain Ms Denning."

"At what stage is your thesis?"

She looked up sharply, apologetically, "Well, it's at the proof-readers."

"But it's complete?"

"Yes, of course. My supervisors are Professors Arthur Harding, Matthew Martin and Dari Züvich. It's almost ready to go to the examiners."

The board cast about, glancing at one another and nodding slightly, until the chair raised his hand and gave her the floor.

Over the next 40 minutes Mike listened abstractedly, noting more of what she failed to say than what she did say. Some things the board didn't need to know yet, but the way she presented her argument the transition to full realisation when the time came would come as no surprise to them.

Basically what they should know at this point is that people were not only traversing the leaky wall they were starting to form small communities and villages across the escarpment, gardening and farming in their own way and self-sufficient, but posing no threat to the regime and taking little from it in the form of sustenance. Her research showed that per-capita expenditure in that cohort is significantly lower than normal, especially in the health sector, but the causes are not yet fully understood.

He watched the screen in front of him, her voice picked up by the audio system as keywords flashed by and entered into the global search engines, providing them all with commentary and review of what she was saying in virtual real-time. Some of the results came up somewhat odd; at certain points he knew well reflecting age-old garbage-in garbage-out results, while others posted advertising for related products and services, but overall her score was excellent without letting too much out into cyber-space. He thought later maybe it was better for a lot of people's personal stuff to simply not appear there, and she was already good at it.

It had been a late meeting, not starting until after 4:00, and they'd spent the whole day in his office going over maps and updating intelligence. What she'd said to him privately is that their riding was not merely to confirm the boundaries but to extend them, for the young people to challenge the old order and see how much further they could extend their territory year after year without anyone noticing. The outer boundary was being stretched by as much as 5-10 Km a year in some parts, and at that rate they now effectively controlled some 60,000 square kilometres, six million hectares of new growth forest and rejuvenated open woodland. In all this time he was the first outsider to know about it.

The moment she finished, with barely a word they were dismissed and made their way out into the corridor and along toward the elevators. Ten minutes later they were down in the subway and on a train heading back west toward the coast, and in 25 minutes Mike had his key in the lock of his apartment door.

The boys had been home from school for several hours. Tempi was in the kitchen cooking their evening meal, and tidying up as he worked with washing in the sink and food scraps in a large bowl ready to be thrown out. Ajani was out on the balcony, leaning out over the rail and crying a shrill, raucous, "Kaarrk, kaarrk, kaarrrk, kuk kuk kuk kuk kuk at the top of his high, pubescent treble voice, from deep in his throat with his larynx bobbing, only partly nasal, and as Mike approached him a bird about the size of a large pigeon flashed suddenly past. Another came up at speed from below, and almost immediately the pair circled over the neighbouring rooftops and together swept past once again before disappearing.

The boy turned to him, eyes bright and smiling. He turned facing the sky a moment, and leaning out again looked up and down, but then shrugged and brushing past went back inside.

As he followed him in through the balcony door the three of them were watching him, but all he did was take Ajani's arm and sat him on the settee, and sat beside him.

Eventually the boy asked, glancing sideways at him, "What?"

"The question, Ajani, and not just to you but the three of you, is not whether you're Gerald or Ajani, if you follow me, but why are you Caplin? I have the Dennings and Tans OK, and I know Caplins - my mother is a Caplin - but what makes you a Caplin? There's a gap there and I'd like you to fill it for me."

Melanie started forward but he held up his hand to stop her, while Tempi at the kitchen door just stood staring at him, eyes wide in astonishment.

Eventually Ajani said softly, almost inaudibly, "De Gruen River mob, boss. Long time before. Dreaming time, *Nyangumal*, *Palykumu*, all finished, that mob."

He waited a while longer but the boy said nothing more, and as he leaned slightly forward in askance Melanie said simply, "They took the whitefella's name, Mike. The survivors. They all settled on Edgingarra and Niminbah Stations and drove cattle for a living, became stockmen, and took the owner's name. It was a very long time ago, you know, over 200 years. His real ancestor is Boniface Djubalmun Stockman. That man was the most senior magic man around the station country in those days. There are song lines about him, they go walkabout and sing him up, that man. The real Caplins are important people too, so we just don't talk about it anymore. A lot of other things have happened since then that are more important to us, and, like, he doesn't need reminding of it."

"He has to have a proper surname to enrol in school, that's all," she went on, anxiously now. "Yes, we know who you are but, I mean, his name's Ajani. It's not Gerald, that's just my little joke, like, among us, sorry about that. He's not gay either, he's good; he really is."

Sitting back, he stared out the big picture window awhile, until nodding slightly he turned to Ajani and asked him, "So, what do you want to do with the peregrines? They'll be nesting soon, I bet they're looking for somewhere. Do you want a box out there for them?"

"Ah, not there, eh? On our balcony, like, me and Tempi; outside our room, all right."

He glanced at Tempi, still standing there just outside the kitchen door with a tea towel in his hand. He flashed his eyes shyly at him, head down, then half turned away swivelling on one foot with the other knee up slightly, tongue in cheek, and as Mike nodded his assent he simply turned fully and went back into the kitchen.

Mike glanced down again at Ajani, sitting there head down in respect, not looking at him, so he rose and scruffing his hair as Bede had done crossed over and went into his bedroom to strip for a shower. Melanie came in with him and did likewise.

Less than ten minutes later the two boys were in the bathroom naked with them, and Melanie turned from scrubbing Mike's back to gaze in askance at them.

"Um, like, we need to know how to adjust the taps. It's too hot, like, the water, unna."

"Hang on a tick, OK, half a minute," Mike said.

The moment Melanie finished he turned to rinse himself clean then gently pushed her out of the spacious cubicle, and turning the taps off invited the boys in with him. Standing back out of the shower stream, he slowly turned both taps on together, the cold just ahead of the hot, until one hand under the flow and more or less satisfied he took Ajani's hand and held it there too. The boy nodded and glanced at Tempi who did likewise.

Melanie was there again, unnoticed by him at first half back inside the shower cubicle staring as intently as the boys, paying as close attention, causing Mike to look at the three of them there now as if they were small children with the same naïve innocence and intense curiosity about every little thing that could be imagined. No wonder they were smart, such quick learners, just soaking every little thing up in their stride, entirely mindful and capable of completely focusing all their attention on tiny specifics.

Abruptly Ajani pushed her out again and glancing quickly up at Mike, took hold of his arm and turned him around. He held his arm up and ran his fingers down his left side, fingering the scarring and each of the bullet marks one after the other, up and down; turning his head toward Tempi to lean closer and look. Then he stood back a step in the enclosed space and turned him around once again, fingering the thick dark hair covering his chest and back; comparing his own slender, hairless, pubescent body with its lucent honey-brown skin and strong muscle definition, with soft, jet-black down beginning to appear over his pubes, while Tempi at the same height and weight was yet plainly a boy, with finer build, reduced muscle tone and a thin residual layer of puppy fat. Beyond that they might have been twins.

Ajani stared down for a long moment at his big man's cock and full scrotal sac then looked up again, gazing intently into Mike's eyes to hold them enquiringly, then with a rapid glance around at Melanie and an odd frown pushed him out too.

"All right, got it now, eh?" he said quietly, then absently stood aside for Tempi to stand under the stream of water and wash himself.

Chapter Twelve

Their next trip took weeks in planning and obtaining permissions, to travel and to access the people they wanted to see. The red tape was tangled and complex, firstly with Mike having to go through his company which acting on a peer-to-peer basis had to obtain permission from both Centre.com and Health.com, and Melanie through her Uni.com status separately, until on advice the two applicants would be travelling together they had to go through the entire process all over again with Food.com and Uni.com putting in joint applications for permission to travel.

The mess was finally sorted out by Stan Fergusson, applying pressure through his contacts with the City to downgrade their catering status if somebody didn't stop fucking them around. They in turn sent their IT guys down to sort out the console operators, and show them how to process the matter, until eventually somebody happened just at the right moment to lean over and press the right key, and APPROVED flashed on all their screens, suddenly without anyone the wiser. As suddenly a printer by itself in the corner lit up, and whined and complained briefly before spitting out a sheaf of tickets and travel authorisations, then promptly went back to sleep.

All they wanted to do was run out along the railway line in one of the state passenger cars belonging to Welfare.com under the Centre.com corporate umbrella, and spend a few days talking to the various silo people in their scattered camps. In the event they decided to run all the way out first, to the extent of cropping before the desert proper encroached, and disembark at Ed Caston's camp along the richer hinterlands on the way back. If need be they could stop at a few more points but it may not be necessary.

Centre.com of all the state corporations was the most paranoid and secretive. It was the least fun job in the whole of the bureaucracy, responsible for overseeing police operations as well as corrective services and social welfare, so their train was arranged in entirely separated, sound-proofed compartments like the ancient dog-boxes of imperial Britain, way back before the great food catastrophe and the global riots which followed.

On the day it still took three hours from leaving home before the train actually pulled away from Metropolitan East-Central, but finally they were underway. The train was driven by a big, old fashioned yet unendingly reliable type of steam engine fuelled along its eastern leg by cut billets of Yellow Box carted across the Nullarbor by its eastern states twin for the purpose, and at this end by Blackbutt from the southwest, both selected for their great radiant heat on burning and minimal ash residue in the firebox at the end of each trip. Their engineers at least knew what they were about, importing the engine custom-built from the New Soviet Odessa to Vladivostok run, and Mike took due note of the fact.

For all that their carriage was well fitted-out, with a tiny, fully stocked pantry and kitchenette and next to it a shower, then a small toilet. Their seat folded out into a double bed for sleeping, and folded back up again allowed them desk space with full communications capability.

Once the train was rolling and the outer city sped past Melanie glanced shyly across at Mike, and said to him, "This will take a week, like, and my period stopped yesterday. Might as well make it a honeymoon, eh?"

After a long moment he said finally, "We're not married, Melanie."

"Yes we are. You don't get it yet, Michael. You're one of us now and do things our way. I haven't seen you put up much resistance."

"Is that right?"

"Yes, it is. And there's something else I found out. Your old people are Rosses, who married among the Caplins, long before they married into the Barkers. But they married among Ajani's people too, on that side, so you're one of us anyway. You'd be Ajani's cousin, closer. You've got blackfella in you, the same like him. No wonder he's taken to you the way he has."

He looked at her, cocking his head and eyes narrowed, bemused by her cheek.

"I know who I am. Why don't you wait a bit and marry Ajani. He's other side to you, like Tempi on the other side again, you could marry either of them, or fool around with them, the right way, properly, unna."

"Well, yes, I can, and maybe I will, given time. But right now you're my first husband and here I am in a fast, air conditioned and super comfortable railway carriage with you, out in the middle of nowhere for a whole week, with all the trimmings."

She half turned toward him. "What's the matter, boss, can't get it up or something. What are you, celibate, or sterile or what?"

She giggled and poked at him, then climbed onto him and ground into him before sitting back a little to remove her panties and start working on him, and he relaxed and smiled.

Chapter Thirteen

After four days of swaying and clattering and sleeping and lovemaking, and sleeping again, and getting out at the occasional stop to stretch their legs and look around, it was good to get back on with the task at hand finally. They could only take so much Bollinger Special Cuvée and Cullen's Willyabrup Sauvignon Blanc-Semillon, and caviar with croissants and crusty baguettes freshly baked on-train, and rich imported Ile de France brie, and either smoked or fresh oysters and local marron with as much Fat Yak and Little Creatures as they could knock back in the meantime.

In the small first aid cabinet were packets of condoms, tubes of personal lubricant, tampons and morning after pills. Mike was going to have to speak to Stan about his catering rules; this wasn't rationing it was bribery and corruption on a grand scale. Right now he was hanging for a nice thick T-bone and a half-decent red, something with balls.

Some of the other passengers gazed curiously at them as they made their way along the rough track toward Ed Caston's enclave, aside from the obvious bureaucrats along the front section behind the engine, toward the rear of the train pretty young girls and generally fat, balding old men; looking odd out here in the desert. As they approached a pair in formal suits broke away from the others and hurried toward them.

"I say, Mr Barker I presume. My name is Michael Rafferty, Lutz Jameson, representing Mr Caston. My colleague is Seamus Devlin, State Law Office, for the government. Don't mind if we sit in, do you?"

"Do I have a choice?"

"Well, no, if you want to put it like that. No you don't."

"Not much point asking me then, is it?"

"Ah, yes, quite. Your colleague?"

"None of your business, is it? But for the record, this is Ms Melanie Denning, Uni.com. She is my research assistant and cultural advisor, here finalising her doctoral field studies on contract to my employer, Food.com. Your contact is Professor Arthur Harding, talk to him."

Devlin was watching him curiously as he spoke, then leaned forward to ask, "I'm utterly at a loss, old chap, to know how you cracked the access code, you know, to obtain your train tickets and travel authorisations. It's restricted, you must have the correct key sequence to cut through the algorithm. What are you doing here, I mean, really?"

"I said, we are completing the last of our field surveys for Food.com. It's a matter of food security. As you are well aware I am Senior Crop Master with the rank of Colonel, Western Command, and we have been experiencing a series of unexpected security breaches that we need to investigate. We might as well have flown here with our armed helicopter fleet as backup, entirely our prerogative, but thought instead not to disturb the neighbourhood so, and take the diplomatic approach. Do I make myself clear?"

The two lawyers stood back a moment, and about to protest as Mike went on, "Do either of you gentlemen have your security clearances with you? You are required to have at least Level 4 clearance to sit in on our meeting, as you well know, and Level 5 when present during our data evaluation. You realise that until you obtain court orders to the contrary, I have the power to second the train guards as escort allowing me to carry out my statutory duties, and if necessary have you detained."

"I think you also want to explain just what it is you are doing on what is essentially an elite travelling brothel, with no prior clearance from anybody to accompany us."

"I must protest!"

"Yell as much as you want. Ed Caston and I are old friends, if you want to be present as his counsel I have no real objection, but Mr Rafferty representing the state will need to show that he has a case against me, and as mentioned obtain court orders to act against me in this matter. It seems to me we are several hundred kilometres from anywhere, and guess what, Food.com owns all the microwave towers, cables and satellite dishes this far out. We own the railway line too, when it comes to that. You never know, it might take a day or two to get you patched through, but we'll be finished by then."

He brushed abruptly past them with Melanie on his heels, until closer to the main group of travellers near the engine he asked out loud, "Is there a doctor present, and a nurse? Would you like to accompany us?"

Several people stepped out and fell in behind them as they made their way across the broken ground toward the tall grain silos, and passing beneath their long shade made their way along the narrow dusty street among the dongas and makeshift hovels; people in doorways watching them sullenly as they approached while filthy, naked and semi-naked children pushed past them to stand staring wide-eyed among the dry grass, weeds and litter along the road verge.

Ed came out to meet them, standing back a moment to see who it was before stepping forward to shake Mike warmly by the hand.

"Welcome, old friend," he said. "To what do I owe the pleasure?"

"Just catching up, Ed. Recap on that business at the last rice paddy. Not much else."

The old man stepped back a moment, looking past him.

"What are those slimy pricks doing here? And that bitch?"

Mike turned to see the lawyers there with one of the fat social workers now beside them, then turned back and shrugged.

"They were on the train, I don't know. We took the train out. There are pallets for you in the end freight car if you want to get one of your forklift drivers to give us a hand with them; just medical supplies, women's things, new clothes for the kids. I have no idea who these people are, but there's a doctor and a nurse on the train so we co-opted them. They can have a look at your kids while we're here, and your mother hasn't been too good lately from what I'm told. Anything else you want us to look at? Have a chat maybe while they're doing it?"

"Oh, right, you're good Mike, thanks for helping us. Those cunts can fuck off but. Tell them to get back on the fuckin' train, eh. Then we'll talk."

He glanced sideways then at Melanie, eyeing her up and down. "Who's this?"

"Melanie Denning, from the university. She's doing research for us on the security breach; my consultant."

Ed stared him in the eye for a long moment before muttering, "Yeah, whatever. Takes notes for you, does she? OK, no worries."

Chapter Fourteen

The trip back was subdued. The fun had gone out of it. There was an odd sort of delay before the train finally started moving, some sort of disturbance up near the engine, but it was around the bend in the line from where they were and they couldn't see what was happening.

After that they just had a quiet beer, and rifled around in the tiny pantry for something decent to eat, finally settling on frozen hamburgers which they warmed up in the small microwave.

"I mean," Melanie kept saying, "they think we're elves. They think we are witches and hob-goblins, lurking in the forest? Like, that's what those silly bits of stick and string, and animal skins, and crosses they have up about the place are, aren't they. They are wards against us."

"And paedophiles - 'pettafiles' - stealing their children? No, I just don't believe it. They're all loonie; inbred bloody hill-billies, except living out on the flat. And their poor children, they're all filthy. They don't even know how to bathe, or wipe their bottom, or dress themselves. Snotty-nosed waifs, when there's plenty of good food and everything humans could possibly need. Tell me this is a bad dream, Mike, and soon we'll wake up and the world will be back the way it was, the way it's supposed to be."

Chapter Fifteen

Granny Tan answered the door when they arrived home. She'd come over to look after the two boys while they were away, and chuckled happily in welcome as they came in the door. Ajani was watching them intently, then abruptly smiled to himself and looked away.

Tempi had an overnight bag packed and was ready to go with his Granny. She wanted to get back so Tempi's parents could go away for the weekend, and there were his younger sisters she needed to be with while they were gone. Melanie looked about and made a quick decision to go with them, and stop off at her mother's since they lived close by; maybe return sometime over the weekend with a few more of her things. As Tempi and the old lady made their way out into the corridor she spun on her heel without putting her bag down, and giving Mike a quick peck on the cheek followed them out the door.

Ajani crossed the room and took his bag from him, and carrying it into his room placed it on the bed. Coming back out he took Mike's hand and led him quietly into his own room, and finger to his lips stood next to the window and moved the curtain slightly aside. He turned to bid Mike come closer, opening the curtain a little wider so he could see too.

He'd placed a flat wooden tray out there, filled with sandy gravel, in the middle of which was a small bowl-shaped indentation with four brown speckled eggs slightly smaller than a hen's egg. As they watched one of the falcons landed, and folding its wings hopped down off the balcony rail, stepped carefully over to the eggs and settled onto them.

Ajani looked up into Mike's face, his eyes glistening with awe and joy, and held his gaze for a long moment before taking his hand again and leading him back out into the lounge.

"See?" he said simply.

"Yep, I thought you would. I thought you'd do it. You're a clever boy. What's next, do you reckon? How long will they take to hatch?"

"Ah, 'nother month I reckon. We'll be right, plenty of pigeons out there, plenty of tucker."

He looked at him. "Want to go fishing, you an' me? Plenty of light left. Catch a big dhufish, eh? Go over to Norman's place and pick up some gear, and go from there, orright?"

Mike nodded, smiling, and still dressed in fairly rough traveling clothes merely waited while Ajani changed out of his shorts and t-shirt into jeans and a bush shirt, and shoes and socks.

Downstairs the boy led him out the other side of the building than he normally used, and down along eventually unfamiliar streets following his native run through the city. After 20 minutes or so Ajani rounded a corner and stopped suddenly, then stepped back, watchful and alert.

"What is it, Ajani? What's the matter?"

The boy put a finger to his lips for quiet, then indicated for Mike to look slightly around the corner and see for himself.

"Raggy kids," he murmured. "Coppers there with raggy kids, orphans. Social worker there too."

Mike frowned and looked carefully around the corner of the building, then stood back in complete surprise. They were Ed Caston's kids, some of them anyway, who he'd seen himself out on the grain belt only this morning, with the fat social worker clucking over them like a broody hen.

He stepped out and around the corner and began walking toward them, but the woman saw him coming and glaring at him spoke quickly to her police escort who came straight toward him blocking him. He backed off, hands up, and stepping away turned back around the corner taking Ajani by the shoulder as he went.

Half-way along the next block he stopped, stepping half into an open doorway and drawing Ajani in with him. They were clear.

"What was that all about?" he wanted to know.

"What? Raggy kids, like, orphan kids. Takin' them to the orphanage. They take them to the dormitory, to school there."

"What orphanage? We don't have any orphans. It was all arranged. Any stray children go to families, with their food rations and everything else."

Ajani looked oddly at him, frowning slightly. "That's our mob," he said finally. "That mob are rubbish whitefella mob, all white trash mob, nobody wants them. Can't handle them, nobody can. They go to state orphanage. When they grow up they all work for government. That Ed Caston mob make kids for government, all sorted out, rich bastard that fella."

"Eh? What did you just say? Don't bullshit to me, you know me better than that."

"Not bullshit. I don't tell lies. White bastard all work for government, but blame us. Blame us for everything. Our mob, like, you know us. You know us now, you been riding with us, marry my cousin properly. I can see, you two been making marriage, proper jiggy-jig, no gammon. She smiling too much, properly married with you now, so no bullshit."

Mike stood back, stunned by the revelation, until Ajani leaned in close to him and taking his hand pulled him along with him.

"Fishing, boss. We going fishing, eh? No worries, talk about it later. Catch nice big dhufish, I know where to catch 'im, in close; know the right place. I know where that one lives, that fella. Maybe mulloway, trevally, silver brim. Next week we take the boat and go out, catch some cod, snapper, sweetlip, morwong."

Chapter Sixteen

It was late by time they got back. Shy Norman refused to allow them to take a taxi, and drove them out to the coast with all his gear, with his own son Eduard in tow, and dividing up the catch later gave his little brother the nice 15 Kg dhufish he'd caught, and after dropping them back off in the city in his old utility took the two mulloway and the sack of silver brim back home to his family.

Neither of them was very hungry after all the excitement, and they were tired anyway. Mike made them an omelette on toast, with a beer for himself while Ajani made a fruit salad with ice cream for his sweets. They'd have the big dhufish for dinner tomorrow, or maybe Sunday when Melanie and Tempi were back and they could enjoy it together.

Afterward stripping off his smelly clothes he climbed into the shower, Ajani doing likewise and following him into the bathroom where he stood patiently waiting, talking softly in his tired boy's nonstop chatter, until Mike was done and getting out left the water running for him, and he stepped in to shower himself.

Mike was already in bed by time he'd finished, and drying himself off cleaned his teeth and came in and slipped in beside him. Covering his loins absently with a corner of the sheet he simply turned on his side and went straight to sleep.

But Mike didn't sleep well. He was furious, with only the boy's steady breathing and calming warmth beside him finally settling him enough to determine that come morning he'd start pulling a few strings of his own. No more Mister Nice Guy, doing the right thing by everyone, only to be betrayed so fundamentally and so rudely like that. Finally he did sleep, when not long after Ajani stirred and woke, and rolled over slightly to pull the sheet and blanket over him, and adjust his pillow, before rolling back over and quickly nodding off again.

He was up early, just after sunup, and was in the kitchen making coffee when Ajani poked his head sleepily around the door, then wandered over to his room to check on the nesting falcons, and pull on a pair of cotton boxer shorts. He went into the bathroom to splash cold water on his face and comb his hair.

By the time he was back in the kitchen Mike had toast on, and he went through to the pantry for Weetbix and the fridge for milk, and made himself a big bowl of cereal with a generous dash of raw sugar. He sat there eating quietly, not saying much, so Mike left him to it and instead had toast with marmalade and a cup of coffee. Ajani stood again and went for orange juice and two glasses, and still without saying much they shared that.

Eventually, satisfied and ready to start the day, Ajani looked across at him and said, "We go see your uncle, eh? That fella, that old one."

"How did you know that?"

"Nothing. Just makes sense, that's all. What's his name, that old man?"

"He is my uncle, Sir Horace Caplin, Uncle Horrie. He's my great uncle, actually, my mother's uncle. He was State Premier at one time, a long time ago now, then leader in the Upper House for a few terms, but the unions screwed him finally over public service reform. He never forgave them for it."

Ajani gazed shrewdly at him. "He'd be the man, eh?"

"Ah, we'll see. I'll have to ring him first so he'll be expecting me. Want a ride in the 'copter, another ride? I'll get Archie to come across and pick us up."

The boy smiled, and his eyes lit up. He jumped up from his chair and started clearing the breakfast dishes, and in short order had the kitchen clean. While Mike made his phone calls he went to his room to change, emerging in his best clean clothes and clean sneakers with his hair recombed, eyes still bright with excitement.

It was still another half an hour before the 'copter arrived and the pilot called down to let him know he was there on the helipad, giving Mike a chance to dress and get ready, and another half an hour before they touched down on the wide green lawn in front of the sprawling bull-nosed, bush-federation homestead facing the broad white sandy shores and blue waters of Calista Bay.

Chapter Seventeen

"Who's that with you, Michael?" The old man called from the back veranda. "Who's the boy?"

"He's a Caplin, Uncle Horrie. Thought I'd bring him, and introduce you."

"Is that right, eh? Distaff side is he? That lot?" He paused a moment, lifting his head toward Ajani. "Come here, boy, let's have a look at you then."

The old bloke must be past 70 by the look of him, with fine white hair and a neatly trimmed whiskers, a lot like Hemingway, strong and well-muscled with powerful shoulders and forearms, and still on his own two feet. He was dressed in slacks and cotton check shirt, not much different from Ajani where Mike was more accustomed to being in uniform, and wearing a good pair of polished R. M. Williams dress boots.

As Ajani crossed the lawn Horrie sat in one of the garden chairs, and as he approached had him stand in front of him. He put on a pair of reading glasses, and leaning forward took his head in his hands and turned him this way and that, then poked his finger in his mouth and pulling his lips back checked his teeth. He undid his shirt and pulled it over his shoulders, running his hand over his shoulders and neck, then across his chest and turning him around looked at his upper back and shoulder blades. Then hand on his chest he had him take a big deep breath, and let it out slowly while he roughly counted his pulse.

He turned him back around and bent down to undo his shoe laces, but Ajani sensing his next move looked him in the eye and said simply, "I can do it."

In short order, nonplussed, he was standing there in his clean boxers, and when the old fellow flicked his finger he glanced across at Mike, who nodded slightly and he dropped them too. The old man turned him around and one by one lifted his feet and inspected them, before running his hand up his ankles and calves and thighs, then his buttocks and lower back, probing for infirmity as if assessing a fine animal.

Turning the boy back around to face him again he tucked his fingers up under his filling pubescent scrotum and lifting it had him cough, before holding his penis out straight and deftly flicking his foreskin back asked him if it hurt or not; checking he was whole and intact while he was at it, finally making him turn around again and bend over to inspect his bottom; his pelvic floor, and anus and perineum. Last, having completed his physical, he had Ajani walk to the edge of the veranda and turn around and walk back, perusing him up and down as he did so.

"It's OK, son, just seeing what you're made of, how steady you are. You have strong bones and fine muscle definition, nicely balanced, good skin tone, and sound breeding; very well set up indeed, and no longer a boy you'll be an up-and-coming young man. Who's your Dad, and your mother?"

"Bede Caplin, sir. My mother was Ellie Tan. Her mother was a Denning."

"Is that right, eh? Don't know your mother's people. I knew Bede when he was younger than you, still a boy; used to do jobs for me, and exercise the horses. Good steady lad. His mother was my receptionist for quite some time, you know, back when I was in practice. He's your father, is that right?"

"Yes, sir."

Horrie turned to Mike. "Fine people these, better than most by a long way. Pity they're not in line, a real pity, blasted downside of a good hybrid program. We'll have to do something about that before long; getting out of hand, you know. How did you happen to find him?"

Before answering Mike indicated to Ajani that he can get dressed if he wanted, but the boy stood there naked a little longer, right hand resting on the old man's shoulder, head held high watching his face and frowning slightly.

"It's all right," he said after a long moment, interrupting the old man's line of thought. "Our grannies look at us sometimes, if they think we might be sick or something, or have worms, or fooling around with girls when we shouldn't be, or masturbating or stuff, like, you know, what Melanie teases me about; me and Tempi, that's not true. I don't mind if people know about me, except, not everyone is allowed, I mean, to get that close. It's sort of, like, special, and you're not to do it again, ever. Mike's not allowed to either. You can be my granny, that'll be all right, but I'm not a little boy any more I'm my own person. I have my name given to me properly, in the old way. When I say something you just have to trust me that it is true."

"And my name is Ajani, like, I'm not a racehorse. My name is Ajani Caplin. You didn't even ask me that, so it's a black mark against you in my book and you need to understand that if you want to be friends with me."

The old man watched him as he spoke, watched his set face and piercing eyes, and the way the boy smiled gently but firmly at him as he finished speaking, nodding quietly to himself as Ajani bent down to retrieve his shorts and pants, and quickly dressed himself.

"Damned right! Good lad, fine temper. Just what we want. Damn, damn white bastards, congenitally recessive, inbred runty whinging Pommie bloody White Australia shits!" he said, his gorge rising. "These people are our rightful successors, our inheritors, I'll be damned if they aren't! Physically they are superior, but they are intelligent and have a pride and a temperament, exactly what we've always wanted. You can't take their soul from them, you can't control them. You have to earn their respect, like a fine thoroughbred. Just want we want."

He looked suddenly at Ajani again, face flushed and eyes blazing. "How many of you are there, son?"

The boy looked confused a moment, until Mike answered quietly. "There may be tens of thousands of them, all up. They control by default the entire southern region, if you want to know the truth of it. They are spreading out under the forest cover, year by year, riding out on horses and marking their outer boundaries."

"Is that right? Well, well, I'll be damned. Is that right, eh?" Horrie stood and turned suddenly, and glanced down at Ajani buttoning his shirt back up, and back at Mike.

"Tell Bede, Michael, he can move his people into the Dwardagin district. You know where. It's a long way out and it's safe, we have plenty of land out that way. Do it quietly; let them take their time, we'll keep an eye out for them. Then move your headquarters into the old homestead on the Coolong property, will you. If you need the placed fixed up, let us know."

Then he turned back to Ajani again, and bending down helped him do up the last button. That done he touched his cheek lightly as he rose and took him by the shoulder, turning him toward the end of the long veranda, pushing him slightly ahead.

"OK, that's done, you came up well. Got something for you too, son. You're a rider, you can ride. Let's see what you think, eh?"

Ajani resisted, pausing a moment to tuck his shirt properly back in, then did up his fly and buckled his belt. The moment he finished he glanced up at the old man's face, and taking his hand started off with him.

Mike followed them through a large shady arbour covered with pink Coral Pea onto a broad open space they'd seen from the air, lined on either side by stables. Horrie stopped there and turning to Ajani said in a low voice, "Son, to be frank with you, keep your black mark against me if you're inclined that way. I owe you an apology. I've been a frustrated old man wielding too much power for far too long, taking too much for granted, and you've reminded me of the proper way for humans to behave. So, think what you like, no strings, eh?"

"What?"

Instead of answering the old man turned him toward one of the stables, toward one of the half doors with the top open and a finely sculpted chestnut head with black mane and dark intelligent eyes looking out at him, ears pricked up, wide even nostrils snuffing enquiringly in his direction.

Ajani froze in disbelief. Horrie stepped across and opened the bottom door, and taking a lead down off its peg clipped it onto the tie ring of the animal's leather halter, and with a quiet voice led it out of the stable.

"What is it first, young fella? What breed? Tell me."

"Arabian, sir." He paused, looking closely. "But he's imported, from Saudi or somewhere."

"Hamilas Rafiq, out of Nazeer by Hamilas al Zalam. He's yours. Do you want him?"

Ajani was speechless. Instead of answering, after a long moment he turned and pushed the old man slightly away, and taking the lead from him walked the exquisite stallion out a few paces, watching it carefully. He led him around in a wide circle and back again, then spoke softly and the horse stood for him. Ajani reached across and touched it, caressing it as it steadied, then abruptly sprang in one smooth leap onto its back. The moment the fine horse steadied again he leaned sideways slightly with one heel into that flank and the horse moved with him, then he repeated the movement the other way. Quickly he had it at a canter toward the track leading down to the beach, but stopped and turned about before they got there and simply trotted back.

They stopped there and stood for a long moment, boy and horse getting a feel for one another before Ajani slid from its back and lead in hand walked around Horrie across to where Mike was still standing near the leafy, pink-flowered arbour. He took his hand and pulled him down level with his face, and said softly into his ear, "Um, like, I don't know what to say."

"Don't you like the idea? Too soon? Too much responsibility?"

"Ah, Mike, don't even ask me that. I can't even say things like that, I'm only a kid. It's all too much. I don't know what to think."

He paused for a moment, then went on, "the old guy, your uncle, I mean, he's something else. I never met anyone like him in my life. What am I supposed to say?"

Mike straightened up, looking as if we going to say something to him about being a man now, but spoke instead across the space separating them, "Ah, you know, Uncle, he just doesn't know what to say. Just for the moment. It's all a bit too much."

The old boy cocked his head slightly, a wry smile on his face, then nodded.

"We'll send him across to Coolong for you then, with a few of our mares. Let's know when you're ready, when you're all settled in, and he'll be there. We can come to some arrangement later. See how you do first, eh? Would you like that?"

Mike gave Ajani a nudge, who turning to face his new granny directly took a deep breath and said simply, "Yes, please. Thank you, sir."

"Done. No worries. That's a good start to another day. You've made an old man very happy, son, and that's no mean trick I can tell you."

"Right then," he went on suddenly, "Michael, that Caston prick, make it look like an accident, eh? Take a few of them with him if you can manage, but make it look like an accident. Not too much, mind, leave room for doubt. Give them something to worry about; send a message if you know what I mean. We'll cover it for you."

He walked away at that point, back toward the house.

As he passed by he turned and added, almost inaudibly, "And that pretty gel you're fucking, the academic, do the right thing and tie the bloody knot, there's a good chap."

Chapter Eighteen

Tempi and Melanie were already back. Tempi was in the kitchen carefully chopping the big dhufish into thick cutlets instead of filleting it, and setting four aside he carefully wrapped the remainder in clear film and placed them in the snap freeze.

It was right on dinner time so they didn't say anything much. Melanie was busy making up a courgette salad to go with the fish, with scorched capsicum, cut asparagus, olives, spring onions and grape tomatoes tossed in leafy Italian parsley, with a dash of olive oil and fresh verjus. Ajani wanted to make some mashed potato with spring onions, and with the go-ahead busied himself peeling spuds. It didn't look as if he wanted to talk to anyone just yet, he'd been dead silent all the way back in the helicopter, causing even Archie to glance across at him to see if he was OK, though nothing forthcoming simply shrugged and concentrated on his flying.

Mike said little himself and set the table. The moment they were all ready for him Tempi simply fried the dhufish steaks with a dash of butter in a big skillet, and squeezed lemon over them before serving.

The food was divine and took up all of their attention, until halfway through the meal Melanie wanted to chat, and talk about the day, and their plans, except nobody wanted to answer. Tempi glanced curiously between Mike and Ajani and back again but said nothing. Eventually Mike, trying to return small talk, suggested that the seismologists were predicting an earthquake season this year, and they might have to pull their operations in closer, but Ajani butted in as suddenly to tell Melanie she had to stop fucking with Mike and marry him.

She sat back, astonished. "Bloody little shit you are," she said to him finally. "You can't fool me like that. That's an earthquake?"

Mike turned on him. "That's not your business, Ajani. You shouldn't have said that. We're not going to start playing your silly word games about my personal business, and hers, then be angry with her when she does it to you. Say you're sorry, all right."

Ajani sat there staring back at him, eyes glistening, but didn't say anything.

"Well, tell everyone the news about your new horse then. If you won't apologise get off the subject at least, show some manners. You're better than that."

Tempi glanced up sharply, staring directly at Ajani and holding his gaze while Melanie sat back frowning, looking intently at one after the other. "What's going on?"

Mike returned her look, curiously. "First, what do you know about the state orphanage? What do you know about it? We ran into some of Ed Caston's children in the city yesterday afternoon, who they were blaming your people for stealing. They came in on the train with us, did you know that? That's what the delay was. Tell me what's going on."

She didn't answer straight away, but gazed out the window for a long moment before turning back to him. She took a deep breath.

"Mike, if we're going there, it's work not home talk, OK? Can we talk about it tomorrow, in the office maybe? I'll brief you fully then, it's political need-to-know territory. We can go over the rest later. Right now tell me about this new horse."

Glancing back in Ajani's direction she asked him directly, "So, who gave you a horse, tell me, I want to know that."

"My new granny," he replied after a short cautious pause. "Horrie Caplin, he gave it to me, as a present. We can go and live out on

Coolong too, if we want. We can move our people into the whole of the Dwardagin if we want. He likes us."

"Horace Caplin? Sir Horace Caplin?"

"Yes, Mike's uncle. We went to see him, ah, about a few things, like . . ." But then he looked across at Mike, hesitant, and fell silent once more. Suddenly he stood and pushing his chair in started clearing the table. Tempi rose to help him, the two boys abruptly separating themselves from the grown-up stuff while Mike and Melanie sat quietly watching them.

"That's where it is, is it? That level? That's deadly serious," she said finally. "All right Mike, no offense, but I'll go back and stay with Mum for a while."

He simply cocked his head, thoughtfully but knowingly.

Then she asked him quietly, "Do you want to marry me? Just tell me now, no obligation, we can call it quits if you want, and thanks for such a nice time. It was great, really, and I'll never forget. If you marry one of our girls I'd be very happy for you both, and we'd still be family."

Mike leaned forward and took her hand. "Yes, that's not an issue. Sorry it's tangled up with the job right now, with business, but yes I would like us to be married. We can arrange a date when you're ready, and do it properly. To be brutally honest Melanie, we've been told, basically; it's the best thing right now, and in the longer term. Is that OK with you?"

The two boys had stopped what they were doing and were standing there silently staring at her, frozen in time it seemed.

She hesitated a moment, then said, "Ah, well, I started to think, like, just another night, give me tonight with you, but I won't, it's still fairly early I'll go home instead. It's OK, let's make it early spring. I'll have a mid-semester break around then, and you won't have started harvest, so that'll be good."

Nobody said anything for another ten minutes or so, and the boys went on with the washing up while the two adults sat, not saying much. Then Melanie simply nodded and rose from the table, and without looking back went into their bedroom and packed her things. After a while they heard the front door open and shut.

Getting out of the boys' way while they finished cleaning and tidying the kitchen, Mike made his way into the lounge and sat watching television for a while. Nothing interesting on he turned it off again and went to shower, then went thoughtfully to bed.

Eventually he heard the boys showering, talking excitedly to one another until they too went finally to bed.

When he woke next morning, however, they were both in his big bed beside him, tangled like a pair of puppy dogs and dead to the world.

Chapter Nineteen

Next morning at breakfast Ajani had a new swagger to him; the new man/boy, head subtly up and chest out. Tempi was standing straighter too, imperceptibly taller. Mike glanced their way briefly and smiled to himself, busying himself with fruit juice, dry toast and coffee.

"Mike," Ajani wanted to know finally, "that granny, he's a doctor, right? Why isn't he called Doctor? Why is he Sir?"

"Because he's not a doctor he's a surgeon, or used to be. One of our finest ever. Doctors don't operate on people they diagnose them and treat them. Surgeons do the operation. It's a separate tradition, and they're called Mr, not Dr, same as barbers. What I mean is, they are licensed to use sharp blades on people, to shave them or cut them if they need to operate, but a doctor has to do the diagnosis first."

"He's called Sir because he was knighted. He did a lot of good things for the country, not just training surgeons. He's a great man."

"I thought he was a general or something, that one; your boss," Tempi interrupted.

Mike glanced curiously at him, cocking his head, and said finally, "That's his brother General Sir Dargie Caplin, my grandfather. He was killed in West Africa. And yes he was my boss, first, but now General Chen is the boss. All right?"

The two boys turned and heads together muttered softly to each other in their boy's way, and cleaning up their dishes and tidying the table finished the washing up.

Kitchen clean, glancing back toward Mike Ajani said to him, "We're going over to Norman's place, all right?"

"Sure, what's up?"

"Nothing. Family business, unna. Ah, maybe we stay there tonight, school tomorrow. See you tomorrow, eh?"

Without further comment they left, closing the front door quietly behind them.

Chapter Twenty

The extraordinary board meeting wasn't going very well. It was fractured, disjointed, in crisis with wholly new and unexpected developments before it which nobody had had time to consider, or investigate beyond their early morning agenda handout not given them until early after lunch. It was to their credit that nobody had blown up, or stormed out, but remained calm, attentive and thoughtful.

The elephant in the room was their corporate contracts with the hereditary landowners, those who had secured their entitlements back in the early days of the colony, and held on to them as their lifeblood and reason for being. Nobody was going to shake them loose. They had met and consisted with Native Title holders and formed a common bloc with them which was now over 150 years old, since the late-modern, post-industrial era when the challenge for government was rather to contain its own bureaucracy, guarantee supply and limit sovereign risk; at a time when food supply came under the control of the big minerals and energy conglomerates.

Population had held steady, not declining after the 9 billion peak in the late 2040s, but neither had it leapt, and for 100 years now the status quo had been maintained almost unaltered. As Stan Fergusson and Art Harding addressed the board and its variously seconded committee members seated around the huge table, Mike sat wondering that the really big issue they'd failed to foresee wasn't the broken down perimeter wall and the kids getting out to play, but the new population, or what Sir Horace had obliquely referred to as the hybrid program.

What had that been about? What were they going to do with them all? How were they going to displace the now aging and decayed state bureaucrats from their all too comfortable tenure, short of mass redundancy, and murder?

Somebody must have been reading his mind. As Peter Jamieson rose to speak the door opened and a secretary entered, quietly circuiting the room to whisper in the chairman's ear before doing the same circuit back out the door and closing it behind her. Stan had covered the current state of politics while Art spoke about the social and demographic makeup as it stood. Peter was due to recap on the prospects in cropping and livestock; none of that unexpected or out of the ordinary, but then it would be his turn to reassure the board on security and frankly, right now he was at a complete loss.

The sudden silence invaded his thoughts and he glanced up to see everyone looking at him. He raised an eyebrow and shrugged slightly, flicking his right hand in askance, face impassive.

"It appears some of your problem may have been solved for you, Mike," the chairman said calmly, almost as a matter of fact. "There has been an accident involving some of your people."

He leaned slightly forward to throw a switch on the console in front of him, saying to Peter Jamieson as he did so, "If you don't mind Peter, we'll get back to you in a moment."

The big screen lit up along the side wall, causing those along that side to swivel their chairs to see it. A reporter on the scene was telling of the horrific vehicle accident in which a number of local children playing on the side of the remote country road had almost been killed by a convoy of silo workers travelling along it, which coming around the bend at speed veered off the road at the last moment to avoid them, crashing down an embankment.

71

As she spoke the camera panned across what looked like the remains of a children's cubby with toys and debris on the side of the road, and on the other side the twisted wreckage of several vehicles.

Mike held his hand up signalling that was enough, and turned asking whether the dead had yet been identified. The chairman flicked the big screen off and read from the small console screen in front of him.

"Your man Caston, it seems. Dead. His wife Marjory and second son Melvin. Dead. His older son Edward Jnr is coming in on the air ambulance with head and neck injuries, with significant brain damage. Six other men are badly injured. Those old vehicles of theirs, you know, entirely unsafe. Is there a liability here?"

"Anything you'd like to tell us, Mike, anything you may know? Our condolences of course, he was a good man, served the company well from all accounts."

Mike sat there stunned, his head spinning. Eventually he replied in a low voice, "Ah, I do apologise. This is entirely unexpected. I'm shocked, ah, do you mind, I'd like to move that this meeting be adjourned until tomorrow, same time. I'll brief you fully then."

"That seems reasonable, and expected of course. Do I have a second to the motion?"

Peter raised his hand and was accepted, and the motion put was passed unanimously before everyone simply stood and gathering their things trooped out.

Mike sat there a moment longer, deep in thought. This was indeed unexpected, unplanned, and he'd better get to the bottom of it fast, or at least take control of the situation. The chair sat watching him, but all he could do was shrug. Stan came back into the room, and as he stood to leave approached him to shake his hand in condolence. He thanked him, but as soon as they were out in the corridor he quickly took his leave and rushed off.

Within 20 minutes he was through his front door, but the boys were not home yet so he went into Ajani's room quickly to inspect the falcons nesting outside his window, and cast about for a clue as to his designs. There was nothing. He was just back in the kitchen taking a cold beer from the fridge when he heard them come in, but took down a glass from the cupboard without saying anything to them, and was pouring himself a drink when he turned around and they were there.

Ajani stopped abruptly. Tempi almost bumped into the back of him. The three stood gazing at one another.

"What's up, boss? Home early, eh?"

"Yes, there was a bad accident. I thought you should know about it, some of your friends were involved. I saw them on the television. Playing on the road it seemed, building a cubby house by the look of it, and nearly got themselves run over."

"What? No, they been told not to do that, those kids. Too dangerous. Might get run over."

"They all right? Anyone get hurt?"

"Ed Caston was killed, with a few of those silo people, his wife and son, another one in hospital badly knocked up. Their vehicles ran off the road and down a bank trying to avoid the children. I was wondering if you knew how the kids are, and what you might know about it."

"What? Nothing. We been at school all day. Like we said, went to Norman's. Slept there last night, eh. Then we went to school."

"OK, I believe you. I can't not believe you." He leaned forward, thoughtfully. "Better talk to Bede then about moving onto Coolong straight away. There's going to be trouble. Maybe have all your people disperse into the Dwardagin quick smart, stay out of sight."

They both stared at him, not unkindly, brows furrowed as if looking down at a hurt animal and not quite knowing how to comfort it, until Mike realised with a shock that they already had everything in place, working to their own plan, fulfilling their own destiny; that Horrie Caplin had merely given them the final go-ahead.

Chapter Twenty One

The loud thrumming clatter of the two gunships flanking him and the deeper air-chop of the big passenger freighters following weighed heavily on his thoughts. Before he'd left he had arranged for Granny Tan to come over and look after the boys. Melanie had arrived with her, unsmiling and not looking at him. But this was his job; what he was paid to do, and he did it well.

Below along the railway he could see the afternoon train steaming along, and knew who'd be on board. This time he had a full platoon with him and a team of counsellors and a relief crew, knowing there'd be trouble. With Ed Caston gone so suddenly a huge power vacuum yawned before them all, creating all sorts of difficulty for a great many people, and he had to move quickly to secure the situation.

By early evening he had the last of the men with all the women and children safely moved to the company barracks just inside the north-east wall, set apart from the city proper by market gardens and orchards, and little Permaculture blocks with their ducks and chickens, and goats and pigs, and small Shetland ponies. The freighters had been out and back, working during the night to air-lift the cottages and dongas in, interrupted during early evening by the train arriving with lawyers and social workers in protest, but the crew had their orders and completed the job under armed guard.

Mike left everyone in the care of his doctors with orders for complete medical reports on each individual, and the nurses once they'd been examined to be showered, drenched and deloused, and dressed in new clothes before sitting down once they were done to a decent nourishing meal, probably the first in their entire lives. Before leaving he doubled the perimeter guard.

Returning home late there was a cooked meal kept warm for him in the oven. As he ate Melanie came and sat with him, not saying anything, while Granny Tan kept the boys in check, not saying anything to him either. She had them showered and in pyjamas while she was in the house, and to early bed.

Melanie finally held his arm, and leaned her head on his shoulder. The moment he finished his meal she stood and taking his plate went to the sink and washed it, then wiped the table and tidied up. He sat in his own thoughts, not looking at her, until finally she took his hand and led him into the main bedroom, stripped him of his uniform, and pushing him backward onto the bed made love with him straight away, urgently and without restraint. Afterwards they showered, but then he made her let go of him and drying himself with his own towel tucked himself into bed. She sat awhile brushing her hair and singing softly to herself before snuggling in next to him.

On his desk first thing next morning were court orders for the relinquishing of state wards into the care and control of the government, which he didn't dispute. They had no complaint about his doing his job of ensuring security and exercising proper duty of care toward those affected in such tragic circumstances, and while none of the adults wanted to stay at the barracks either he let them all go. They were picked up in plain charter buses running on biofuel, and disappeared down the road.

The prefabricated cottages and assorted dongas and out-buildings were company property, however, made available at the time as an apparently misplaced act of charity. Once the people had taken their personal possessions with them he kept them at the barracks to be fumigated, stripped and refurbished. He had an idea to refit them entirely, and air-lift them out into the Dwardagin to be put to good use finally. Of far more interest were the medical reports and lists of names, though he would have to wait weeks probably for the tissue and fluid samples to come back from pathology.

Before he got into the pile of reports he picked up his phone to order a grader crew out to clean up around the silos, get rid of the remnant building debris and accumulated rubbish and reseed the area with native grasses and shrubs.

PART THREE

Chapter Twenty Two

Their daughter Louise was born the following spring, properly legitimate and according to form, though doted over incessantly as the months passed by Ajani and Tempi taking turns to carry her around on their backs, in a traditional sling Granny Tan brought over for them. Two nestings of falcon chicks had both long flown, and a third was being set. Tempi had turned the kitchen and lounge balconies into herb gardens to catch the sun, while between nestings Ajani had planted their bedroom balcony to native flowering shrubs.

Granny Tan made up a cot in the main bedroom where she slept while Mike was away, taking it in turns with Melanie to attend to the baby if need be during the night, and throughout the day while the boys were at school and Melanie was lecturing and tutoring, except they had to do their homework of an evening. She was strict about it. On weekends they went over to Norman's and either swam in the river or went fishing or crabbing along the foreshore when the moon was up.

For Mike is was a blessing to have his household running normally, with people in it and a coherent routine. He was constantly away now. His world had turned upside down and a whole new security infrastructure had to be created around the spreading and emboldened tribal peoples let loose from the sprawling perimeter suburbs, cutting their way now through the wall itself and making new, properly formed roads in and out. Most of them were now doing well, shifting their gardens and piggeries and chicken runs out onto broader acres, but others had formed into gangs and kept their city habits, especially the more resentful, sword-wielding adolescents. It was his job now to mould them all into a disciplined fighting force; a formal boundary patrol replacing the old furtive, game-playing silliness.

The bigger task ahead was to renegotiate their agricultural leases. Nothing could be properly put in place until that long-winded process was complete, and the landlords ruling Landsraad sensing a far greater independence from the unproductive and dysfunctional state were proving to be intransigent. But first things first.

Waking from his reverie he glanced out the window at the gunships flanking him, two on either side. Reports had come in of a plantation in the deep forest out beyond their old boundary which required investigating. As they made their approach the two outer helicopters broke off and began their broad sweep of the area using infra-red and colour analysis to see if they could find any more, transmitting their data in a steady stream directly to Jamieson's iVEX-B as he followed them in real time by satellite imaging, while Mike with his two escorts made a sharp descent and swooped in on the clearing where the plants were growing.

There was a shed there and men were running from it. He didn't bother with them; they heard him coming. The horse patrols would pick them up in the bush. He had better things to do, and focussed instead on the screen set in front of him. Something was odd about this job that wasn't making sense. It went undetected for too long and it was only after a new patrol had been sent into the area that any report had come back to them.

Bede rode out from the edge of the clearing and dismounting waved up at him. Archie did a quick dip and turn leaving the two big clattering escorts on-station while he hovered briefly and touched down, dust and sticks and leaf debris swirling up around them.

The horsemen had dismounted and had three captives trussed with rope, their guns in hand. It was plain from their dishevelled look and manner they were remnant Castons; from one of those families. The moment Mike was beside him, without a word Bede took a pistol from one of his men and walking over to the three captives shot them dead. Then taking one of the men's' rifles he turned and shot his own man, and as he fell dead another standing close by, then a third in the shoulder, merely wounding him. Stepping over to him he turned him roughly around and undid the katana lacings and took his sword and scabbard from him. He did the same with his two dead horsemen, and standing before the assembled men raised the three swords high above his head before handing them over to Mike.

"Right! Listen to me," he said finally, "no more bullshit. The rest of you boys in that stupid fucking Musashi gang, learn a lesson. Miyomoto Musashi was a legend, the finest two-sword fighter in history, not a dumb-arse street fucking hooligan. You are now disbanded. Each one of you will buddy up with one of the forest boys, draw straws for partners; anyone but a brother or first cousin, but no more drugs and no more smart-mouth adolescent crap."

He stood back a moment, addressing them all, while Mike stood formally at ease, giving his immediate subordinate the ground. "Anyone at all found with drugs or illicit alcohol; mull, coke, speed, crack, smack, heroin, meth, eckies, anything, will be shot where he stands. There will be no questions asked. Your families won't even get condolences; don't even think about a pension. There will be no formal announcement of your death, and there will be no funeral. Your body will be dumped out in the forest somewhere for the wild dogs."

"Be very careful about your own partner, keep a close eye on him. You'll be sharing digs with him until your service contract is done and you're free to go home and marry. You'd better get to know him real well; sleep with him if that's your inclination, because if you fuck up he's the one who will execute you. In a fire fight, he's the one who will cover you, and save your life."

"Am I understood?"

"Yes, sir!"

"Right. I will not repeat myself. The good news is, you will be allowed to keep your katanas, but you will all receive advanced training in swordsmanship. We have a master coming in from Japan to supervise training, Master Gorō Kunitsugu. You will receive new rifles, and advanced marksmanship and sniper training. You will learn martial arts, properly this time. You will be fitted with new uniforms and wear the emu feather plume which will identify you. You will be given new horses, not all at once but as our breeding program develops. You will be our new light horse regiment, patrolling open country now as well as the forest. You will be called the Dwardagin Light Horse. You will form into companies, and you will be exemplary."

"Is that understood?"

"Yes, sir."

"Right, settled," he said more quietly, before turning to the wounded man. "You," he said to him, "come with me."

Chapter Twenty Three

"Congratulations on your promotion, Brigadier," the chairman was saying, though Mike nodded merely in acknowledgement. The compliment had a jagged edge to it.

"Still under General Chen from all reports. It will be business as usual, I trust?"

"As you know Charles, Beijing has a seat in the Landsraad, as does Djakarta. Their presence there is only ever fruitful. Our relationship is longstanding. Your own people will tell you that."

"But don't you think you're overdoing it somewhat, old chap?" Stan Fergusson interrupted, to the full glare of the chairman. "We are talking three full battalions, are we not?"

"Not quite three battalions, a bit over two and a half; only 2,600 men. They cover more than 150 million hectares of new- and old-growth forest and prime farmland, now that they've had the go-ahead. They range over the entire southwest from Badgingarra down to the Blackwood, and out to Wyalkatchem and Jerramungup. The psychological passive containment scheme failed; the conditioning and the Happiness Purpose, you know that very well. The new system provides jobs, and discipline, and adventure. We're replicating it in the Kimberley and Northern Pilbara, under Brigadier Ngaringkinjarri. His people are here for training as we speak."

He sat back. "Our projections are for higher productivity with fewer social costs, and a wider variety. Pork and chicken, and fresh vegetables especially, will be more readily available. There will be more fresh fruit, and more of our crop land can be set aside for biofuel production, with a lifting of the moratorium on engine fuel finally. We'll be installing more oilseed digesters at our silos, and back-loading the end product to the coast. There will be more trucks on the road and more independent operators, and more boats in the water. But that's not the problem, is it."

"Care to elaborate?"

Mike leaned pointedly forward again. "We have stopped the child abductions, is what. And the corruption and kick-backs and drug trafficking. Your problem right now, not ours, is the queers and the eunuchs and the Mandarins are strapped for cash and the bureaucracy is about to collapse. Our catering contracts are not being met. The state is bankrupt."

"Order, order please, gentlemen!" Charles cried, banging his gavel. "I will simply not allow this board to deteriorate. If we have no further business to discuss I declare this meeting closed. Mr Fergusson, I will see you in my office."

Chapter Twenty Four

His phone was ringing and he hurried to answer it. It rang and rang, urgently, but the moment he reached for it it stopped. He looked at the display. It was Melanie. He tried ringing her back but the number was engaged, then suddenly the phone rang again.

"Yes, hello. Mike."

"Mike, finally. Ajani and Tempi have been arrested. They were picked up by police on the way home from school and found to be carrying crystal meth, enough for a long weekend party and play. It's not possible. Where would they get that much, and why would they?"

He paused for a moment, then asked, "Are they OK? Where are they being held?"

"City lockup. Bede is with them, and your solicitor, Hamish Drummond. Ah, Mike, there is a witness apparently who says he saw the boys dealing. It doesn't look good."

"Is that right. Well, we'll see about that."

"No Mike, stay out of it. Keep your distance, OK? I just rang to tell you. Come home as soon as you can, they'll be out later and we can talk to them then."

When he arrived the house was crowded. Granny Tan was there with her older son Yuen and his wife Sophie; Tempi's parents. Norman was there too, and the air was electric. Mike glanced about, then went to the fridge for a cold beer, asking the others to join him but they all politely shook their heads.

Around 6:00 pm the front door opened and the boys were there, Bede close behind. Their faces were pale and drawn. They didn't say anything either, except Ajani walked straight up to Mike and pulling him by the shirt sleeve led him into the bathroom with Tempi and Bede close behind, closing the door behind them. He undid his trousers and let them fall, then lowered his briefs, cocking his head slightly at Tempi to do the same.

"Look, Mike, those coppers poked their fingers up our arse. Said it was a strip search, and they had to examine us. They kept doing it, in front of one another. Look what they did."

He turned around and bent over to show what had happened to them. Ajani's anus was red and inflamed, while Tempi's was bruised. He'd fought, his arms and backside also bruised. Ajani stood up straight again, pants and undies around his knees, and said, almost in a whisper. "Don't say anything. Nobody's to know except you and father, and Norman. Not ever. Promise."

Mike thought for a moment, standing there looking down at the boys, and finally said, "OK, I promise, we promise. Take your clothes off and have a shower. I'll have Granny bring in some fresh clothes for you. There's been no bleeding, no blood in your underpants or shorts. She won't know, not about your bottoms anyway. I'll take your gear to the laundry and put it in the wash, OK? They've just been rough, deliberately, to insult you. When you've finished your shower I have some ointment, you can put it on yourselves. You'll be right."

He glanced at Bede, standing there face grim, and nodded slightly to him. Bede went out and with as slight a nod at Norman they both left, closing the front door softly behind them. In their passing all Mike could think was, by God those people can move silently when they want to.

The boys stripped and handed their clothes over, and got into the shower. Mike took it all out with him and not saying anything went straight through the kitchen and placed everything in the washing machine. He turned to Granny asking her to take them clean clothes, then passing the fridge took a fresh beer and went into the lounge to face the family.

"Ah, they'll be right," was all he said. "They're young men now. Not little boys any more."

Nobody else said anything, until finally the two emerged from the bathroom clean and tidy, in clean clothes and their hair neatly combed.

Knowing what was going to happen next, they both sat obediently at the table and for the next half hour skilfully fended off every question, Ajani eventually cutting the proceedings short by announcing suddenly that anyway they were moving out to Coolong, getting out of the city, too dangerous these days, for kids.

Next morning, breaking news on all channels showed extended camera footage of a grisly head on a spike outside police headquarters, identified amid wild speculation on political motive as that of popular BDSM host and sex partner of prominent LGB member of the state parliament, Simon Rindos. The rest of his body had been found behind a rubbish skip three blocks away.

Melanie rang again about 11:30 to let Mike know that the charges against the boys had been dropped.

Chapter Twenty Five

Ajani was right, Mike decided. During exercises he'd held long meetings with General Chen and his northern counterpart Walter Ngaringkinjarri to form an entirely new mounted regiment under the Commonwealth Regional Security Treaty.

In the entire West, after all, while the rest of the planet hovered steadily at around 9 billion people, here there were still less than 4 million. It wasn't population that was the problem but the sheer extent of the land area of 2,530,000 square kilometres, close to 100,000 square miles. They would stake their third part-battalions to create a combined regiment to patrol the Gascoyne as well, and with air support cover the enormous expanse of desert. Minerals with Energy.com, and iVEX with their Tanami Wide Field array, were all happy to share their security infrastructure, and engineers and intelligence units to help defray operating costs. The vast inland desert and its attendant mineral fields had always been independent-minded, and would side with them anyway it goes.

They had to get out of the city. It was the 19th century American Civil War against the landed families, and the Russian Bolshevik Revolution against the Kulaks and peasantry, that had sent the world on the wrong trajectory. Their earlier 18th century revolution followed by the French Revolution, and Sun Yat-sen's fight against the warlords and corrupt cities, the courts and civil administration, and here we are all over again.

Administratively it wasn't the kings who were the problem, but the courtiers; the eunuchs and queers and public service Mandarins, or so they styled themselves. Their problem could be stated as a vain effort at normalising their own ideas, reifying their own policies, institutionalising and setting in concrete their own limited view of the world for others to follow and obey. It was a real problem because apart from the side effects their forms could not keep their shape in the real world for long enough and from so far away to have any real effect, and they blamed everyone else for the damage.

Policy melted quicker than it was cast, with no time to set, and in their anxiety to prevail they forced the routine order of things. The other big hurdle they had yet to overcome is what to do about The Inheritors, as they styled themselves; the apparatchiks and party bosses who'd taken control of preselection and with it the parliament and the executive, and with it again their own bureaucracy. The old Unification Party had long ago formed a coalition with the Feminists and the LGB Party and their corporate affiliate Sex.com, determined in the name of social equality to entrench monocultural, monolingual social engineering as the cultural and political standard.

It failed because they refused to acknowledge difference, and to marry out; over two centuries causing in-breeding and propagation of recessive genes which they all wore now as a badge of victimisation, except where the more affluent among them managed to bring new semen in from somewhere to artificially inseminate lesbian couples and make a great show of raising ostensibly normal, healthy young men and women to eventually take their appointed seat in the parliament, and act as media icons for the party faithful.

The Landsraad had been formed in response among the great landowners, long ago buying up and amalgamating abandoned small farms as the long rural recession due to climate change and prolonged drought bit hard and people were forced to migrate and adapt as food security became a serious issue, and the Food Bowl concept developed. They had to protect themselves more than anything from the moralising, ill-informed policy directions of government and worse ministerial caprice that on top of everything else had almost destroyed the northern cattle industry and with it their established export markets, and brought cereal and oil-seed cropping to its knees, and near-famine to their northern neighbours.

He had to sit and think at times, now that he had Bede out commanding the southern field and had time on his hands, whether he was being obsessive or merely recognising a need to plan well ahead, and understand what it was he was embarking upon. Access to the best communications technology, and subscriptions to every reputable peer-reviewed journal on the planet, gave him the most accurate information and reliable commentary that could be had. He spent hours in conference with Melanie and Art Harding, and Peter Jamieson when he could get him away from his mainframe, going over with them his hybrid genealogies and gene maps; assessing for the first time their common multicultural policy of maintaining the distinct groups, and only ever marrying out to produce a hierarchy of select breeders and this army of F1 and F2 hybrids with their strict laws on interbreeding, sexual relations and marriage, and oddly it seemed their tacit acceptance of homosexual levity especially among the adolescents. The end product he decided to consider his stud book.

After they moved house out to Coolong Station he spent as many hours again out riding, and talking boy talk with the boys and their friends, and swimming with them and being an uncle to them. And coming home again to make love with his wife, and nurse and play with his little daughter, and laugh and say nice things day after day to Granny Tan. It was nice because they had worked out a way to keep work and home entirely separate, which appeared to be a gift these people had in knowing intuitively the proper context for each of their many different, ostensibly contradictory behaviours.

Ajani was right. He had it sorted. Mike began to see old Boniface Djubalmun the Stockman in him, and what he'd been on about that

90

made that old Myall blackfella both legendary and at once an outlaw. Horrie Caplin was the one who'd awakened it in him, that day, the first time in his life the boy had been met with raw personal power, and even in his favour had been so overwhelmed by it he was lost for words. He'd earned for himself a fine horse in the transaction, but in doing so came to him for reassurance. There was something in it that disturbed him.

He decided finally to simply change his recruiting system, and without saying anything to the Food.com board took his plan to the next Security Council meeting with Walter Ngaringkinjarri and General Chen.

They both agreed with him.

Over the coming months, and especially during the school holidays, they gradually took all the children out of the city, keeping only some of the houses so their people could come and go nonetheless, and let the rest go. They built schoolrooms and dormitories on Coolong and on the surrounding farms and outstations. At the close of the academic year after she'd finished marking all her essays and exam papers, Melanie then advised the university that next year she would not be renewing her teaching contract.

She gave no reason, but her plans were to establish new ethnic schools for her people. Mike retained his city apartment and slept there when he needed to, but spent more and more of his time in the field; based variously throughout the Dwardagin while Ngaringkinjarri in the far north did the same thing with his own people along the broad Fitzroy River Valley, from there linking up too with the East Kimberley and Territory Side mob.

Chapter Twenty Six

These northern boys were pretty sharp, not the same as the southerners and looking more like Burmese with their mixed Asian-Aboriginal blood where his people had a lot more Chinese and Caucasian in them and more lightly tanned. Mike guessed the tribal elders had sent these boys off to serve in the new bush militia, like the old mob down this way, and kept their own at home with them to out-marry and secure their traditional alliances and rights to land. He'd wait and see, he thought to himself, who showed up at the next Landsraad.

No matter. They passed muster in good order and he could see their commanders were proud of them. Coming south for joint exercises had been a good idea, establishing their flash style and competitiveness before taking final steps toward establishing their combined Gascoyne battalion and settling finally on regional headquarters and distribution of staff. These boys were superior in bushcraft while his own were much better riders and light infantry. He had no doubt either that before too long some of his own boys would being going north, into the far Kimberley, but he'd wait until the dry season was properly underway and the hot steamy monsoon behind them.

Slightly annoying to him right at this moment was that with the three northern companies here the older children couldn't contain themselves. They refused to attend their classes, but rode their horses about endlessly chiacking and showing off; Ajani on his fine Arabian stallion in the lead with Tempi and his friends riding the mares. They made a fine sight, he had to admit; the formal march-past with its flanking outriders was spectacular, but they were mucking around too much.

It was a good thing, he thought wryly, they were not yet allowed to wield swords but waved their wooden practice *boken* about from horseback in wild abandon.

He leaned forward slightly to speak quietly to Bede, who half-turned to listen. "What we had better do with that wild kid mob," he said, "is form them into a cadet unit. Some of the older lads can act as their corporals and sergeants while they get the hang of it; get a bit of close-order drill into them and tidy them up a bit."

In the event Ajani refused to follow orders, and Tempi was with him. He refused to join the cadets and refused his place in one of the new platoons, even when they offered him a single chevron with the rank of Lance Corporal. That made it worse, he insisted. Now people would really think he was just another useless gay-boy bloody suck-hole.

He wanted to continue working with the Rajput horse master Horrie Caplin had brought in from India, and become a stud master and horse master in his own right. Jitendra had been a Sipāhi of the Greater Persian Military Forces serving in what had once been Northern Iraq and Kurdistan, and Georgia and The Ukraine, and knew all about mounted cavalry tactics.

Ajani said almost as an aside that Mike should take him on as his batman, and he and Tempi would serve as orderlies. And anyway, he was going to study biology and anatomy and livestock husbandry at university, and veterinary surgery he added after a moment's furrowed reflection.

Instead, on making his own enquiries Mike learned the man had been a ranking officer and after long talks with his men, to keep him close Mike commissioned Pratap Jitendra Singh with the field rank of Brevet Major under Colonel Bede Caplin and assigned him to his personal staff. It was not a decision he was obliged to make but he chose too, partly to satisfy the obligation he felt toward the boys and partly because it provided them with a broader opportunity. Ajani was a shrewd schemer, rarely overdoing it and always with a good outcome. In the long term, having an impartial and unrelated officer standing entirely outside their complex kinship system was a wise move on his part, and it did not go unnoticed.

His residency could be sorted out as they went along, and the moment he was cleared promote him to full rank, though with reciprocating exchange with India and the calibre of sponsorship at the level of Landsraad it was more a formality at this stage. In the meantime he would continue working with the horses.

The matter settled he put his mind to better things. He still had to complete his full report to Food.com, which through their various memoranda of cooperation would find its way in short order to the land lords and to the parliament and others as a matter of course. He had to tread very carefully. Rumblings within the city of treason and insurrection were already being heard, and those pricks were just as likely to panic and stir up public hysteria, and with it civil unrest against them. It was a good thing the state was flat broke right now, though with food shortages brought about more by delivery breaking down than empty silos and depleted stores that could make them even more dangerously bitchy. He had to maintain his tight intelligence network throughout the inner city and sprawling suburbs through Norman's people.

Coming in under his radar, what he hadn't quite guessed at the time when he might have was that the move provided Ajani and Tempi with a ticket to the Landsraad. In payback they were no longer to ride around chiacking and showing off with the other kids, which brought the slightest of smiles to Ajani's face before taking Tempi's sleeve and turning away in case it was noticed.

Chapter Twenty Seven

The phone kept ringing and ringing, and he reached across to switch it off. The staff meeting was almost done. His intelligence on Jitendra proved more than satisfactory, and his residency and officer's commission had come through Government House, except they promoted him to full colonel ranking alongside Bede.

The door opened, however. "Sir, pardon the interruption, but you'd better come."

He glanced up, then turned back to the table. "Gentlemen, seems I'm required. Do we have any other business, or anything we can leave until next meeting?"

Bede said quietly, "State wants the Metropolitan Police to take care of security at Landsraad. Should we deal with that now?"

"They'll be bringing in TRG as their own bodyguards, won't they? We get along pretty well with those fellas. We can do the same job for our people. All the police will be doing is crowd control, fending off the protesters. Let them have it."

"You might like to keep Norman and his boys on their toes," he added as afterthought, then no further response he closed the meeting and stood to leave, packing his brief case as he did so.

Chapter Twenty Eight

Peter Jamieson rushed to the door. "You're here! Mike, dear chap, someone you absolutely must meet. Arthur sent him across. We have a problem. You do need to know."

But the two men already knew one another.

"Paul," Mike said straight away, shaking him by the hand, "very long time. How are you?"

"Fine, no worries. Needed to emerge from seclusion eventually, you know how it is," the other replied cordially. "It was Uncle Horrie, actually, gave me a call."

Mike turned to Peter. "Ah, this is my cousin, Paul Molloy; old gentry stock. His mother is a Caplin, but from the respectable side; down the Caplin line direct, not via the Rosses. Purebred you might say. We went to school together, except he went into banking."

Peter looked blankly confused for a long moment, as if trying to absorb the idea of people being related to one another but failing miserably.

"Whatever, as the case may be," he muttered eventually, then glanced about as if trying to recall the purpose of the meeting.

"My office?" Mike offered.

"Yes, indeed, surely, that's it. Come along, then."

"Paul, what's up," he asked, once they were settled with coffee and traditional shortbread.

The other gazed thoughtfully at him for a long moment, sipping his coffee before putting his cup down and leaning forward to take a biscuit.

"What you've managed to do, Michael," waving it about, "is burst their fucking bubble. That's what's up."

Mike stared at him a long moment. "What?"

"Everyone has gone bush, and now there's a housing glut. The market has collapsed."

Peter leaned forward excitedly as if it were obvious, and he had the answer straight away, but to Mike the question was entirely opaque.

"What has it to do with us? Housing? What are you talking about?"

"The state had a scheme going, dear boy, that's very old now by the way; well over a century in fact, after they let everything to the big corporations. Their main business has been transport, roads and housing, and increasingly of late entertainment as you have no doubt noticed. All their housing tenants' children are essentially state wards and their parents classified as foster parents on permanent welfare."

"As you know, since the climate changed the economy has been in more or less permanent stagflation, held in balance by welfare spending from your minerals and energy, food and water royalties that held demand up artificially high enough for a dilettante sort of ennui to set in, but not much else if you know what I mean."

"Go on."

"But the key to stability is residential housing and commercial property. The real estate cycle is longer and more stable. With the wall around the city and a captive consumer market on more or less fixed commodity prices, they've always had a long enough response

97

time to keep things tweaked. But now you've gone and upset the proverbial bloody apple cart."

"No, Paul," Mike said finally. "Nothing to do with us. Their idea was to maintain spending and stimulate demand, without worrying about what the money was spent on, or whether people actually wanted it. It was all psychobabble; Happiness Purpose with a captive democracy which was so fucking boring eventually turned everything finally into sex-parties and drugs. Buildings are no longer being maintained and commercial properties and road works have deteriorated, like the bloody wall itself."

"There is no fault on our part. Instead of being sick on processed junk food people went back to growing their own fruit and vegetables, and keeping pigs and chooks, and finally went bush."

"Ah, but, precisely so! The point being, they were still living in houses and still paying their rents. Now they are not."

"No, the rents were getting too high anyway, for hovels. The market was held up through their own valuation, depending on how much rent they wanted to charge. Nobody was actually buying or selling. There was no market appraisal. Then they allowed dirty money in from Russia and China to prop everything up. All they wanted was somewhere to launder their money, and they did it by buying houses here in the West. They bought into struggling businesses too, or set up their own, then went bankrupt after a couple of years wrote it off on their tax. The people simply walked away from it all finally, once they had somewhere to go."

"Another thing, Paul," he added after a long pause. "Don't worry about the real estate. It's all speculative. The production cycle is going to be far more stable because we have people back living back in the landscape. They'll be living in new houses and running their own schools, and working for us, paying us rent, except

98

productively and sustainably. It's no economic collapse, just a demographic shift. The state don't like that because to them it represents a power shift."

"Their Food Bowl idea with vast nature reserves and no people in them just didn't work, it created welfare dependency not full productive lives. We worked it all out. The banks shouldn't be worrying, they will have far more substantial deposits backed by productive use of land, not centralised credit and debt cycles controlled by the city."

"But the state will argue that it's the one state, Michael," Paul broke in, fully ready to argue his point. That's what he'd come to do. "Constitutionally they are the government. It is a power shift, and they're not too pleased about it. What you're doing is Medieval. Way back then there was good reason the crown acted so against the old barons, and the clans and the *tuatha*."

"It's not a State bloody constitution, Paul, there's no such fucking thing. They are constituted federally, under the Commonwealth, but don't have the guts to secede. So they play these stupid, petty little games all the time, thinking way over here nobody will notice."

Peter interrupted, excited now, his brain running at high speed and not just from the caffeine. "I say, chaps, the pair of you, best get our heads together on this, what? Better get a few more brains working on it, a bit more synthesis, so to speak."

He turned to Paul. "Are you free, my good fellow, for a day or two? Good."

"Michael, you can fit four into that helicopter of yours? Well done. Right then, we'll pick up Arthur, I'll call him straight away, and get our jolly little brains trust out to Coolong. We'd better have a jolly conference among ourselves before Landsraad."

Chapter Twenty Nine

Everyone sat stone-faced, looking blankly at him. Melanie leaned over and said softly, "Mike, you simply cannot discuss this business in open forum. It's not for public consumption, it's properly sacred business; it's private, dreaming business. It's Law. We call it bijnitch."

"So what do you want us to do? How are we to go about it? We have to do something."

"You better come bush with us, eh?" Ajani broke in. "Not that fella, only you. We fix it up, no worries."

Two days later Melanie came into the kitchen as he was making coffee and said, "Mike, we'd better go now. People are waiting for us."

Outside they had horses saddled and ready for a good ride by the look of them, with supplies for a few days at least. The ride itself wasn't long as it turned out, but steep and difficult, up over the high breakaway southeast of the Coolong homestead proper and down the other side into a long shady gorge with clear running water and shady trees where they set up camp.

Before long they were joined by a group of old people, from somewhere he couldn't begin to guess, but they were there with Ajani holding one old lady by the hand and helping her over the rough ground. Tempi was there too with Granny Tan. Soon there was a crowd of old men and women sitting close by, and once they were settled some of the younger men lit a fire and took smoking leafy branches from it, and waved the smoke over everybody, chanting softly as they did so.

Once they were done Melanie began to speak.

"A long time ago," she said, "my great-great-grandmother Valerie Denning married what was then called a half-case Aboriginal, whose father was Chinese. His name was Eddie Tan. She was a doctor, you know."

"That was a time when a lot of the people were living in fringe camps, and on local rubbish dumps, when government started building houses that none of them wanted to live in. There were other people too who'd been stolen away as children and were working for government, the same back then as it is now. It was a time when people were deeply divided and arguing among themselves. Fifty years later they still couldn't get people to live properly in houses, and that was the time government started to evict them and because the fringe camps had gone people lived on the street, or were sent to jail. Most of them were in jail at some time or other."

"That time, that 50 years later time, a lot of Chinese started coming to Australia. Not the old Chinese but the new Open Door Chinese. The first of them were students, but soon workers were coming too, then more of them when the Chinese Government started farming in the Kimberley. You know about that part. In the city, the street people were fighting with the new Chinese street gangs, and the African gangs except they stayed separate. It's us we're talking about. We didn't want to be Blacks, like Africans and Americans, because we're Australian; we have our own way. Outside on the streets people were fighting but in prison they helped one another, because of the mostly white guys in there, you know. That's how this bijnitch started."

"What happened was the Caplin mob, your mob but on that side, were a bit different because up on the station country the owners looked after them like family. That was the proper Caplins, and they took their name. The station life wasn't all bad, people aren't all bad.

101

Some of them had married Japanese and Chinese, and Indos and Malays, you know, from the old pearling days."

"Sir Edward Caplin, in those days, was pretty sympathetic. He started a scheme where the boys coming out of prison could go and work up in the station country instead of going back on the streets, so they could learn to ride and muster cattle, and take pride in themselves. He was a doctor too, but he had good political connections. When the mining took off and there was a lot of money around, other people started other sorts of schemes, but our boys really only wanted to ride horses and muster cattle so the station jobs were most successful."

"What Valerie Denning did was persuade the women that they should be marrying out, to the Asians and the older white people who had adapted to the bush, the old Scots and Irish. They couldn't live in the city either, not very well. She and Eddie had a good family, three boys and two girls, who did well in their lives; in mining and cattle, that sort of thing. She started marrying them off to the station people, the Caplin mob. When it started getting buggered up because the young people were marrying anyone they wanted, she laid down the law. She went over into the Territory to learn from the traditional people still living there, and they taught her about the old ways. When she came back across she just told everyone how things were going to be, and the old ladies agreed with her."

"So, these old ladies here now are the proper law keepers. They know all the genealogies going way back nearly to when the whitefella first came here. The old men here are the senior lawmen. Nobody can discuss this business without them being present. Nobody can get married unless they approve it first, except now they use Asian terms and do things that way because it avoids the old conflicts. But people have to marry the right person. They can fool around, but only the right way or they'll be punished. Their brothers and sisters will beat them up."

She leaned in close to him. "See, husband, you didn't have a choice and I didn't either. It was just lucky Art Harding introduced us; I was trying to think of a way to meet you, and there you were. It's no joke. Another thing is, only our clever people are told the truth. Ajani and Tempi are clever boys, they will be the most senior elders when the time comes. They are good boys, the best we have. You are being told all this because you need to know, but you must swear to keep it to yourself. You cannot be a boss of this business, but you can be a custodian as we say, so you will never be told everything; not like Ajani. If you betray us you will be killed, no matter what else. This is the most sacred thing to us."

"Horace Caplin is the other custodian, the only one ever before you. You should know that. He calls it the hybrid scheme, and we let him think that; doesn't matter. What matters is he likes us, and helps us a lot." She turned slightly to indicate one of the old women. "See, that old lady with Ajani is Bede's mother. She is Ajani's granny, properly. She's the one. She used to work for Horace Caplin, and he taught her a lot of things. She is more like, our sort of technical adviser, on genetics and things like that. Now you know."

"Everyone else is told stories," she continued. "If a Caplin boy is to marry a Tan girl, they are only ever told what good people the Tans and Caplins are: everyone else is rubbitch, no good for you. So when they're growing up all they think about is marrying a Tan or a Caplin. Caplins and Dennings, or Tans and Dennings, the same thing. What's important now is we are past critical mass, and the thing has taken off. It has its own legs. It's not so hard anymore, the culling has stopped; we don't have to be so strict. It's become our culture, our way. It's what identifies us."

103

"Why it's important, Mike, is now we are out of the city each mob will have its own country, its own places to look after. We already know; that's what we've been doing all these years. It's all back together now, not buggered up any more. When we get back we'll show you the maps; actually they are in the paintings on the walls at home, except Ajani will show you how to read them properly. But you're not to talk to anyone about what he tells you, it's our secret."

She watched his face intently, until he said quietly, "I'm not one to tell you your business, and I'm honoured that you shared it with me. But, one question; if you all continue along that same path, eventually you will inbreed like the whitefellas. There are a lot more of them then you, many thousands of times more, with a far higher risk. How do you answer that? Just so I know."

She turned to glance around at the old people, who were smiling at him, bright-eyed as they'd smile at a child bringing a top report card home from school. He was clever, this one, properly. As one they all nodded slightly and Melanie turned back to answer the question.

"Well, first, they're mostly city people, those Wedjala; nearly all of them. We are bush people. They just made us live in the city, around the fringes anyway. Those old fringe settlements are what eventually became the outer perimeter estates where the Vietnamese and Chinese had their market gardens, when they built that wall around everything. In all this time, nearly 200 years, we didn't breed with Wedjala. We still didn't marry Djanak. While they were all just fucking we still bred out. We weren't only going out through the holes under the wall, we were meeting with people from up north. All those boys had been in prison together, you know."

"That's the idea, Michael. Breeding out, not in, but it has to follow the rules. Like, Dennings can marry out more to Caucasians;

Tans can marry out more to Asians; and Caplins can marry back to the blackfellas, except, the person has to be somebody. They have to have a family and a genealogy we can follow, and present themself to our way of thinking. The old people will do a thorough check before they allow it. Ethically, I know it's a dilemma, and we can be accused of a lot of things not just murder and assassination, but we are breeding out the rubbitch. That was the choice forced on us, or continue living like dogs."

"And another thing, Mike. We don't just speak English. We can speak Chinese, and Thai and Vietnamese and Hindi and Malay and Indonesian, and the Aboriginal languages over this side. We can speak European classical languages too. English is rubbitch, it's not a language it's a common tongue. It steals words from anywhere and cobbles them together, like the English do everything. It's like their society and culture, it has no spiritual integrity, or beauty, or depth. That's what Granny Valerie was really on about, and that's how she persuaded Granny Edward Caplin. She was a Sufi. In our way, during the ceremonies, we call her Granny Sarai, and we call him Granny Ibrahim. Eddie Tan we call Granny Lot because he was the one who led our people away from Sodom. The difference for us is the boys are not to be circumcised, and girls are not to be cut or mutilated. Women and men are equal, and the body is God's will. It is already holy, the way it is; it is the Temple. That's why we don't say Abraham."

She looked away, into the far distance, searching for words.

"All that Granny Mob, all our people love them. Everybody loves their granny so much," she started again, but then stopped abruptly and after a long pause started singing, a small song that was joined one after the other by the old ladies, and as it grew by the old men. The song went on all day and all night, and for the next two days and nights while Tempi and Ajani with some of the younger adults with them did the cooking and made sure everyone was fed, and took turns at keeping the song going while others stopped to nap, or to relieve themselves.

Then on the fourth day, early in the morning the old people disappeared again and they rode back to the homestead.

Chapter Thirty

"Where the bloody hell did you get too, mate? It's been a week already."

"Ah, called away. Bit of bijnitch you might say. Sorry, Paul, unexpected. Been looked after all right? I see Horrie's trap over in the shed, he must have driven out to see how things were moving along. No doubt you've been wined and dined."

"Sure, no worries. Arthur's pottering about, somewhere. Spending a lot of time, I take it, with that Pakistani of yours; discussing walled cities and siege tactics and cavalry attacks. Jamieson flew back a day or two ago. Couldn't wait, said he'll pop back out when you're ready. "

Mike glanced quickly at one of his staffers who promptly went to make the call, but then he was distracted by hoof falls behind him and he looked around to see Horrie approach with Ajani on his lovely chestnut stallion at his left flank, and Tempi coming up behind on a roan leading a spare horse. Still mounted, he turned his horse about to meet them. Both boys had showered and changed, now wearing brand new moleskins and wrangler check shirts both with the crease still in them, with gleaming new R.M. Williams riding boots and enormous Territory sized off-white Akubra hats sitting right down on their ears; grinning happily. Properly flash.

He glanced back at Paul. "You ride OK? Want to come for a ride. Seems the boys want to show you around the place."

Chapter Thirty One

"The more serious problem they face, Paul," Art Harding was saying, "is not the housing glut but loss of the most productive labour, the best small business brains. The fruit and vege markets are down and the small groceries are in short supply. All the city has left is the old Anglo-Regency gaming and liquor economy, and behind that entertainment, and prostitution and drugs. The rest is entrenched bureaucracy and packed judiciary to keep honest employment up and with it some semblance of bourgeois respectability."

Mike was barely listening. He'd heard it all before. He sat gazing at Melanie and at the two boys seated close behind her. Of course, she is a Denning, and they are Caplin and Tan, the three of them elect; to be groomed as the most senior elders when their time came. Ajani was by far the cleverest of them, more profoundly attached to the land, but without them he would be in a lot of strife. He was right when he said if Melanie took him he'd die, but in that he'd meant quite as much that if he took Melanie he'd die. If anything came between him and Tempi he'd die.

The new princes, the focus of all unity. He couldn't begin to imagine the burden they carried, and at their age. Simple loneliness was their one big enemy, especially at this critical transition in their lives as they negotiated puberty. They'd profoundly mourn the loss of one another, and waste away. Their people would fracture and disperse.

The room was silent suddenly and he broke out of his reverie. They were all looking at him.

"What, ah, my apology. Other things in mind," he said lamely. "Please go over that last bit."

"Employment," Peter muttered.

"It's not our problem. Compulsory schooling followed by mandatory community service in the form of mounted cadets then rangers; fast light cavalry. Outside those hours, every child has a paid job in the gardens, or at the markets, or a trade pre-apprenticeship or working with the horses or livestock. You all know that, we've shown you around. We have the skills and capital and net productivity to back it up with our own bank, issuing our own currency. There will be no income tax, only land rents. That was the one big mistake they made; they should have followed Sun Yat-sen and Taiwan. What is there to discuss?"

"The city, old chaps."

He sat back, somewhat exasperated, and sighed. "The subject is not interesting to us. Our meat and grain contracts are in place, except we can now provide a wider range of better quality food as well. They can take it or leave it. Our remit is fulfilled. We would much prefer that they opened their markets and established a market economy to mediate commodity prices, and paid their flamin' bills, but that's their problem."

"Anything else?" Horrie Caplin wanted to know.

"No. What else is there? We are not their problem. Singapore and Macau are their problem, and Hong Kong, and Djakarta and Bangkok and Kolkata. They might have woken up to that simple fact two hundred years ago, and oriented themselves toward their own future and left us out of it. The Regions might have been semi-autonomous in a sensible working relationship with them, and they still might, but they've reverted to Regency London; Medieval Rome more like it. It will take generations to lift them back out of the rut, except with our own currency now they'll have to offer a fair exchange rate."

Paul Molloy leaned forward, curiously interested now. "What are you saying, Mike?"

"They refuse to allow the open market to mediate food prices, even though it's illegal. Under the Commonwealth we have a floating dollar. We can leave our new dollar to float. It will find its level against the Yuan on the basis of Asian markets, not the city's. They will just have to wear it. The Kimberley is with us, and that means Indonesia and China are with us. I am still the most senior Crop Master. I trained them all. I have no doubt whatsoever of the situation."

They all sat back. He was right, there was nothing more to be said.

Finally old Horrie leaned forward and said gruffly, "Well, young Molloy. Happy now to run our bank for us? Want the job? Should you accept, you'll be chairman and chief executive of Western Regional Banking Corporation - WRBC. Aside from Professor Harding, the board will consist of Landsraad. Overall administration I suggest to you will be Hanseatic, operating out of our coastal ports where we'll offer independent branch franchises. How's that sound, eh?"

Paul sat back thoughtfully. "We still haven't discussed the housing crisis, and collapse of real estate. What are we to do about that? As a bank, how are we secure collateral against loans?"

"There is no real estate collateral. We own all the farmland. We have all the use entitlements apart from a few ghetto areas in the lower southwest they call The Heritage. The remnant is set aside as state and national parks with co-sovereignty derived from Mabo and Wik between the crown and the traditional owners. Our land is not for sale, and cannot be placed at risk against borrowings. We have no real estate market. There will be no speculation. That's their problem, not ours."

"Fair enough, but that doesn't answer the question. What do you want the bank to do?"

"Managing our overseas transactions and accounts," Mike intervened. "Primarily extending and managing credit to our various merchant houses based on their assets, but more importantly their cash flows and their credit history; their standing and reputation, and factoring services to our subcontractors and small firms. We will treat the city generally as a foreign entity, and aside from our grain and meat contracts we trade with them on the same basis. We will meet our tax obligations federally through rent levies. The state can argue with them about it, not us."

"Landsraad will sort that out, Michael."

Mike glanced quickly at Horrie as he spoke, nodding slightly, then noticing Tempi leaning forward eagerly listening, and Ajani alert, for their benefit he added, "What people will always need is not land, that's out of the question; it's food and raw materials they need. If they want to be productive their proper role is value-adding; making something of what they have not just consuming it, or wasting it, which means education and health-care, and clothing and apparel, and secure housing and trade skilling, and higher education of course. We must be getting our people into university, and graduating in the top rank as far as we can manage."

He turned his gaze from the boys back to Paul, who was no longer listening either. He was keenly watching their eager young faces.

He nodded. "What you've done, you people, is secure a future for yourselves. What you want to do is invest in these bright young up-and-comers, isn't it."

"All right, count me in."

Then he sat back ruefully. "I'll throw my property portfolio in for good measure. It's worth absolute zilch right now - over $1.7 billion down the tube, on paper anyway - but what the heck. You might as well have it, along with the current defaults as they come in. We can sell them as we go along to pay off any residues, and discard what we don't need. Owning a good lot of outer metropolitan land and inner city properties might turn out useful down the track."

"What you mean, boss, people don't need land? What you talking about?"

Ajani was insistent and wouldn't let him sleep; wouldn't leave him alone. Finally he rolled over and said to him quietly, "Different idea, eh? Don't need to own land, as property. Land isn't property. In your way, you are the land, and the land is you. How can you buy and sell that?"

"Don't need it, not like that, so we get rid of the idea, all right. Like old times. What Paul was talking about is not selling the land itself only the land titles, the entitlement certificates lodged with Land.com that give people the right to hold land for themself; to alienate it from the state government and put it to good use. Not everybody needs land, do you know what I mean? They can use the product of the land, and add value to it, but they don't need the land itself."

"What's been happening is everything's being wasted, when value needs to be added all the way up. When people buy anything, then, it needs to be good quality and worth something, not just rubbitch they can throw away."

The boy lay on his back, one hand up behind his head and the other down across his belly thoughtfully fondling himself, staring at the ceiling for a long while, then out the window into the night sky.

"Then people are worth something, eh?" he murmured finally. "Not living on rubbitch tips, too many kids, wrong way fucking all the time."

"Yes, that's it. That's the idea. That's our proper job, Ajani, to make people worth something; to make life worth something. Landsraad is the land holder, and we are the land user. We are the primary producers. Like that."

"That's why we need to find good wife, good husband, eh? Have good kids, you reckon?"

"Yes, that's what I reckon."

Finally the boy nodded and gradually curled up against Tempi and went to sleep, breathing quietly and steadily.

PART FOUR

Chapter Thirty Two

Ajani was far from happy when he was told he couldn't go with Horrie Caplin to Landsraad. He became sulky and fractious, fighting and arguing over every petty little thing, until Bede in real frustration confined him to barracks away from everyone.

Mike went in to see him when he had a moment spare, but he was angry with him. Melanie tried next. She emerged stern-faced and grim, and without a word went over to the stables and saddled a horse for herself. While she was away Granny Tan came to sit with the boy, not saying anything to him as he stared forlornly out the window.

Five hours later Melanie returned in a sulky with Granny Caplin.

Next morning there was a light tapping at his door and Mike went to answer it. Ajani was there. He'd been crying, and hung his head.

"Sorry, Mike," he said under his breath, almost inaudibly.

"What was that, Ajani?" Melanie yelled from the kitchen.

"I said I'm sorry, all right."

He looked as if he'd relapse if Melanie said anything further. It was a good thing she didn't. Mike stood waiting there a moment until he glanced up and him, and catching his eye simply winked, and reached over to draw him in close.

"Big job on, properly, eh," he said eventually, "can't bugger up, all right."

"Need to go Landsraad. Need to be going this bijnitch. No good, something happening."

"Want to talk about it?"

"No, you're bloody well not!" Melanie was close behind him now, furious. She pushed her way past them and out the door, and stepping out onto the edge of the veranda called out at the top of her voice, "Bede, come and get this son of yours or there's going to be big trouble. You hear me? Better look out, properly, no shit."

She spun on her heel at that, and grabbing Ajani roughly by the arm pushed Mike with her other hand back through the door. Bede appeared, but stood there staring across at them without a word. Taking the hint Ajani tore loose from Melanie and without looking back trudged sullenly across to him.

"OK," Mike said after a few moments, following Melanie back into the kitchen. "Want to tell me what that was all about?"

She turned to look at him. "You really are naïve, aren't you, husband. You don't get it, do you? No bloody idea."

"What? I don't get what? Melanie, sorry, but you're just going to have to tell me. If it's so important, I mean, I really do need to know."

"Can't you figure it out? It's in your bloody face. You know they're not really Caplins. Isn't that enough?"

He simply shrugged, hands up, eyebrows raised in askance.

"They are Djubalmun. They are Kadaitja men. Norman is the Feather Foot Man, the Emu Feather Man. Ajani is the worst of the lot. He's far more clever than any of them, ever. They all say the same thing, that he's old Boniface Stockman come back to sort things out. Good thing he's still just a kid right now, and it's a bloody good thing you have him on your side, I can tell you."

"Ah, come and sit down, Michael, OK? I'll tell you the story."

She sat him at the kitchen table while she sat at the head, and reached across to hold his hand, looking him in the eye.

"It's embarrassing." She paused a moment, glancing away looking for words, then back again.

"What you need to understand is that they had you marked for assassination, along with Eddie Caston. If you hadn't been fully armed with your gunships and men guarding that rice crop, you would be dead. The vehicles were just a decoy, but you were too quick and the men in the bush behind them had to withdraw. I think they underestimated the speed you move with your trained men and your helicopters and technology; how alert and well organised you are. They needed to take a closer look."

"We didn't know, our side; us Denning mob. They don't tell us things. Our grannies had you on the marriage list. When we found out what they were up to there was hell to pay. Granny Caplin was furious and she tore strips off the lot of them. Bede is still her son, you know. After that we had to move very quickly. We had to bring you in, make you one of us. It was the only way to protect you."

She paused, watching his face. "Ah, what people don't realise is, Michael, like, we all look the same. Because of the hybrid program, you know. But we have our different temperaments. If a new child shows the wrong temper they'll reassign them, not that often, but Ajani is a serious Djubalmun. They were right about him the first moment, and the Tans had a job on their hands to manage him. Binding him to Tempi was smart. You know what he's like, he's uninhibited and he has no shame."

"He does have shame," Mike interrupted, "but in his own way. He's a growing boy, that's all; raging with hormones and a perpetual

117

hard-on, and relentlessly inquisitive. That's what you want in a strong healthy boy that age. He's too bright, that's his trouble. Today's world is far too boring for someone like him, and you can't blame him for it. What I need is for you to tell me something about their plans, and what they're thinking. That's all I need right now. I need to know what to do with him."

But she didn't know, or didn't want to know. All she would say was Bede's father was still in prison on a life sentence for murder, and pulling a lot of strings from inside. But he wasn't the problem right now. Ajani was the one to watch.

Chapter Thirty Three

Mike was mildly annoyed. Did they all think somehow that he'd won his crown and three pips in a pub bloody raffle? Perhaps Melanie was right and Ajani did need watching, but Ajani was as close to him as anybody, and was trying to tell him something. Men under duress had a way of communicating that women just didn't seem to grasp; though so did the women in their women's way, probably.

She was his wife after all and loved him dearly; not only a brilliant academic but a devoted mother on the way to becoming a senior women's elder. She carried her own responsibility, and did care for him deeply. She had simply not understood that Ajani was not a little boy any more to be bossed around, yet retained an image of him as adult that she'd gleaned not from him but from his older brother, and his father and grandfather, fearing he'd turn out just like them.

With one ear he was listening to the intelligence reports from Falcon Head and the Landsraad venue, but something else was bothering him. There were still over one and a half million people in the city proper with food of sorts but little to entertain them now and not much money to buy things, and the walls were breached. His job was food security and with it rural security, not dignitaries, and politicians and party hacks ready to launch mass protest at the drop of a hat.

He leaned forward suddenly. "OK, thanks Adrian. Get in touch with Canberra on this. You can fly out tomorrow if you like; take your team. Foreign Affairs and Trade can take care of it. They'll bring Defence in. The army can look after it. What have we here right now, locally? State police on crowd control, TRG on personal security? Is there anything else?"

"No sir."

"All right, let's wind this up. Bede and Pratap, stay behind, will you?"

"Ajani, wake up. Come with me."

The boy stirred lightly, murmuring something in his confusion, then sat up wide awake and alert. He stared at Mike for a long moment, eyes wide and gleaming in the semi-darkness before slipping naked out of bed to quickly dress and follow him nimble as a cat out into the faint pre-dawn light, the sky above just starting to glow softly above the breakaway. They went like shadows. Tempi stirred and gazed after them, then rolled over into Ajani's warmth and curling up dozed off again.

Chapter Thirty Four

The apartment had been broken into, not overtly but by experts. Little things were not quite in the right place. Ajani noticed it first. He stopped and turned slowly, scanning the room, one hand up to warn Mike. Mike went to check his security console. Nothing had been touched, so he ran his network log to discover it had been hacked from outside, allowing somebody to simply come in through the front door. Whoever had done it were serious professionals. He nodded to himself and probed further for IP and MAC addresses that told him the source of the intrusion, then with a quick house scan for bugs that came up clean, pushed a USB stick into the port and download the entire log.

There was nothing else amiss, apart from the small items moved slightly about. He had left no files or any trace of his work there. All of his systems were automatically wiped clean to military specification following every defrag before shutdown. He knew his firewalls at Food.com and on Coolong that Peter Jamieson had configured for him, routing all his traffic through the iVEX-A and out of harm's way, were indestructible at 2048-bit encryption.

He glanced across at Ajani and shrugged, finger to his lips, then hand-signalled to him to get what he needed to bring and they'd clear out. He wanted to check his peregrines on the balcony first, but the nest was deserted now so he went to his room and reaching up under his bed slipped a catch and removed a long package wrapped in black cloth. He was about to place it carefully into his school back-pack when Mike signalled him to open it and show him.

He hesitated, pausing thoughtfully before looking about in askance.

"No, we're clear," Mike said softly. "But there might be microphones pointing at us from the other buildings, and cameras.

Come into the bathroom and turn the shower on, OK? We can talk in there. You can show me what you've got."

Ajani moved quickly across the familiar room, package unobtrusively down his body, and did as Mike suggested. Mike followed him in as he knelt on the tiled floor with the shower streaming behind him to drown their voices, and unwrapped the cloth to reveal a fine Japanese 60 cm short sword and a matched pair of 30 cm tantō. Beside them lay a long dagger of flaked black obsidian with an oiled, deeply ribbed wooden handle of spearwood attached with kangaroo sinews and red resin. Next to it was a rough, fairly recent cowhide sheath plastered with red ochre that he could hide in his clothes. The blade was ancient, glistening with menace, for a purpose that was out of the ordinary. He ignored it, distracting attention away from it.

"Wakizashi," he said. "Not tall enough to wield a full-length katana, eh? Or maybe closer fighting, inside. All right, I guess you know how to use them. Anything else while we're here? Want to talk to me about Djubalmun bijnitch, get it off your chest?"

Ajani glanced at him. "Properly cheeky, that bijnitch. Too dangerous. I'm just a kid yet."

"What do you want to do then?"

He looked away, as if into the far distance, and sighed. He stood, then turned to Mike and taking his arms pulled him down to his level, kneeling him on the tiled floor so he could talk to him face to face, gazing steadily into his eyes.

"All right. Properly, no gammon. No bullshit now. I got to let go Tempi. No good for him any more, too serious. He's a good boy, hurting him, not his bijnitch. Sometimes he crying. He wants to be chef. But those old ladies make magic on us, when we are babies. Need to shift across, find another one."

"And that other one is me, isn't it. What's wrong with Tempi?"

"Nothing, he's just a boy. I'm too strong for him, sucking his energy, taking away his cojones, you know. He's got no cogliones, that boy. You saw him, just a pee-pee. His balls can't drop. No bloody good, eh. Better let him go."

"So you'll take mine away, you think."

"No. No, that's not right. You're a big man, serious. Make stronger. Come together, eh, better synergy. 'The sum is greater than the parts', we learned that in school. Like that."

Mike stood and went to the door for a moment, gazing across the lounge room through the long glass window at the mid-morning sky.

"If I make conditions," he turned to ask, "in this binding, do the conditions hold?"

"Yes, no worries."

"All right, first you are no longer to speak that silly half-pidgin, like you're some poor bastard blackfella. You are a fine scholar, highly intelligent and really very talented; way past time you held your head up. If you are bound to me you must speak properly, eloquently. I guess you are already learning the other languages, so you are to speak them well too. That's the first thing. If you slip up, if you lapse, the binding is severed."

"Second, we'll send you to Royal Military College, Duntroon. Don't worry about the horses, it doesn't take that much to sort them out and you're already good at it. So now you'll live with the men in the barracks and work with Colonel Jitendra not me. The binding doesn't mean you have to be in my house, or sleeping with me. You've proved to me you're not just a nice-looking gay boy with a pretty boyfriend, but you're not a little boy any more either."

"Third, I understand bijnitch a lot better than you think. People need to talk straight with me, no gammon. I am a Brigadier in the Australian Army, Western Command under General Chen, commissioned to food security and the integrity of our agricultural districts. This binding is not with the little boy Ajani Caplin, it's with that old fella Boniface Djubalmun. That's the deal. This bijnitch is serious. We have to sort out these Wedjala pricks, those bad-arsed Djanak, or we are at constant risk. Production costs and end waste are simply unsustainable, no worries about the rest of their bullshit. It's been going on far too bloody long. That's the job ahead of us."

Ajani was barely listening. He stood gazing eyes wide into the far distance, as if through walls and walls and walls, out across the land, far back in time. His skin glistened with beads of sweat, and his pants tented with erection. A slight smile betrayed him. It took a while for his breathing to steady, and he glanced quickly up at Mike before turning away.

He stripped off his clothes with uncharacteristic modesty, respectfully, and back to the door stepped into the shower, turning the cold tap on full blast; gasping at the shock before slowly adjusting the temperature to normal.

A few minutes later he stepped out again, more or less restored, and bending down picked up the obsidian dagger before indicating to Mike that he should join him back under the shower.

When he did so Ajani took his hand and slightly nicked the ball of his thumb.

"Not too much, only a little bit. This old blade is too bloody sharp. Proper blackfella magic. Bloody hurts all right, this bijnitch," he muttered almost to himself, taking great care in the way he gingerly handled the glistening translucent black glass, glowing almost under the overhead light among the sparkling droplets of water streaming from the shower head.

Then he nicked his own thumb and pressed it against Mike's to mix the two drops of blood, quietly mumbling something. After a moment he rinsed the tip of the blade and stepped out of the shower. He dried the dagger and giving it a good wipe with the wrapping cloth slipped it into its sheath. He turned then and taking a towel dried himself.

"Is that all?"

"That's about it, eh? That boy's balls going to drop tonight, that Tempi. Catch up quick. He'll be real happy tomorrow, now we let him go, wake up fidgeting. Can't help himself. Burning hot cock, I tell you. The ladies sort 'im out good and proper, pretty girl looking at him already, eh, no worries. You and me, we fix this Gadiya cunt, all right."

Mike stopped towelling himself and stared at him, slowly shaking his head.

"You'll be living in the barracks, eh? No privacy, nowhere safe," he said. "Give me that knife, I'll keep it for you, eh? When we get back we'll put you on full sword training under Kunitsugu, you'll be good enough to start with him by now. The quartermaster will get a new katana in for you, a proper one, made by a sword master. When you see him, let him know what you want and he'll have it made for you."

Ajani cocked his head sideways, watchful and alert, then smiled inwardly and without saying anything picked up the glass knife in its sheath and handed it across.

Chapter Thirty Five

By mid-afternoon Ajani was just another bored and distracted kid on his way home from school, sauntering along with his heavy back pack and Mike in shirt sleeves and slacks carrying a brief-case variously ahead of him, or falling behind to browse the shop window displays. He stuck to the standard routes and pedestrian crossings, stopping mutely when need be for the supervisor to wave him on, until a little way out of the city proper he waited at a bus stop and when the bus came along they both hopped on board.

Eventually they got off, half a block away from Granny Tan's old house, but instead of going there Ajani made his way around the far end of the block and slipped down a laneway running through it. He paused, glancing back to ensure Mike was still with him before opening a door in the wall and disappearing through.

It was dim inside. A few men were there, including Norman and a few others. There was an older, wizened, grey-haired man sitting at a rough table against the back wall. As Mike entered they all looked up. He shifted sideways abruptly away from his silhouette against the daylight outside to stand inside along the wall, pausing briefly to allow his eyes to adjust.

Nobody said much, until he turned to Ajani, cocking his head.

The boy shed his back pack and put it on the table. Looking back at Mike he said, "This one is Norman, you know him. He took us fishing. These fellas, they're cousins, doesn't matter."

He glanced at them one after the other, taking in their features, until his eyes rested on the old bloke against the far wall.

"Ah, that one Basil. Granny Basil; Basil Djubalmun Caplin. He's outside for a couple of days; home leave, you know. No worries, eh."

Mike merely nodded slightly, turning his head away without acknowledgement.

Norman interrupted the following silence. "What job you want done, boss?"

"What's up, first?"

"Ah, some fellas causing trouble. Party bosses, coppers, fucking gov'ment people. Making an army, going to break out. Reckon they can beat us, bring us back into line. Make us come back, run the shops, grow the veges, drive the road grader, collect the fuckin' garbage. No bloody way, mate. We're free now, not going back anywhere, not for those poofter cunts."

"All right, got the picture. Know who they are?"

"Sure, we know. But angry crowd already too big. Going to break out. Big trouble comin', big war comin'."

"Are they mobile? Do they have their field command sorted? Some sort of plan that you know of?"

"All those fellas out along the wall now, camping along the southeast. They'll move any day, go out through the wall there, where we cut the wall. Along there. There's a big mob there now, all ready to go. Their bosses are there, some of them, the rest up in the city. Some, round about the place, you know. We can find 'em, no problem."

Mike leaned back, thinking, then looked up at him. "Do what you need to do. Take out their communications and command structure, is that OK? Don't worry about the rest."

"Sure, boss. No worries."

He caught Ajani's gaze and tossed his head slightly to indicate they should leave now. The boy stalled a moment, then shrugged and picking up his back-pack followed him out into the laneway.

"Take as down along the southeast wall, Peter, will you? Let's have a good look."

He stood back, and with his hand on Ajani's shoulder brought him in close. It was no surprise to him that he held back, the vertigo looking down into the great domed lens of the Live Earth console was enough for any sane person, except mad Peter of course who leaned fully over it ready to dive straight in, eyes flashing back and forth while he checked his bearings and made adjustments, hands moving so fast it was hard to follow him as the image steadied and oriented toward them. Then he brought it up close, to about 250 metres above the ground.

Slowly Ajani edged forward, overcoming his fright at the idea of the thing, until eventually he caught sight of a mass of tiny figures moving about and bent closer to watch them. He nodded slightly, and glanced back up at Mike.

"Where do you reckon?" he wanted to know.

"You tell me, eh?"

The boy looked down onto the earth's surface again, scanning about to orient himself, then asked Peter to zoom him back up. At around 11,000 metres, with his finger he traced the wall itself, moving northerly until he recognised the barracks then back down again to the swampy southernmost boundary where nobody lived much and the wall held firm. Coming back up a little he pointed to the southeast beyond the scarp, and Peter promptly scrolled the image to follow his finger until he stopped him.

"That place," he said finally. "That place, Gwambyrangup, out there on the flat. That's big crop country, not many buildings and pretty open. We can hold the scarp and the breakaways on every side, so we'll have the advantage."

"Why there?"

"We can bring our cavalry against them, hold them there. They don't know the country further out, never been there much, but we know it. They won't go anywhere, they don't really know the ground. They won't go up too close to the barracks either, they'll go around. Anyway that's steep forest country up that way, our country. We know that place better. South is New City. Maybe some of them will go to Landsraad down that way, the demonstrators. No, this mob, they'll go southeast."

"Good teacher, that Jitendra?" Mike grinned. Ajani glanced sheepishly at him.

"So, what's the threat, do you reckon? How do you assess it?"

"Ah, nothing. Big crowd of people, maybe 200-250,000, but they won't have a lot of weapons and they won't know how to use them very well. Lot of women and kids, probably, big protest march. Take Back The Land. They think it's democracy and numbers will win, but they have no training and their supply lines are no good. We control all of that, it's our bijnitch, so they won't have enough food or water. Maybe they're all just stupid."

Chapter Thirty Six

"You did what?"

"No, it's all right, he's reading out of textbooks. And someone's been telling him stories."

He turned to face her.

"How's Tempi? What's going on with him?"

"Oh, you know, he's all right. Bit frisky lately, is all."

"Is that right? He's usually quiet. Testicles starting to drop finally, do you think?"

"Maybe. They're boys aren't they, the pair of them. What are you doing with Ajani? That's what I want to know."

"Hang on, I'll show you something."

He rolled over and got out of bed, and stepping over to his briefcase reached inside to take out the rough cowhide sheath with its glistening obsidian blade and oiled wooden handle. He placed it beside her on the bed, where he'd been lying.

She stared at it for a long moment before looking up at him, shaking her head.

"That thing? Yes, um, sorry I was angry with you. I didn't want to say anything to you about it. You're too smart for me, Mike. Where did you get it?"

"Well, I sort of persuaded him to part with it temporarily, for safe-keeping, since he's bound to me now and will be living with the young men in the barracks, so nobody to look after it for him properly. What do you know about it?"

She nodded slightly, knowingly. "It's a curse," she said, her voice distant. "If the thing wasn't so beautiful, so finely made, so old, somebody would have broken it by now. There's a glamour on it. The boys pass it down. Old Basil held it last . . . you met Basil, a fucking rogue, murdering bastard . . . and he passed it on to Ajani. That's where Ajani gets his chutzpah from."

"Why didn't Bede get it, or Norman?"

"Bede takes after his mother, no time for bullshit, except he'll follow along if you know what I mean. What he needs is strong leadership, then he's definite. I think you did the right thing with him. Norman's sort of, like, not too bright; easily led. He has his talents, but no imagination."

"OK, well, let me ask you something then. Why didn't you tell me all this before?"

She glanced up sharply at him. "What did you want me to say? What did you expect? Our people, you know, only let out what needs to be out. The rest of the time we're all bullshitting at each other. You white people, you can say things straight out, like, because you can get away with it. You have this idea of truth, but what you don't understand is truth hurts. It doesn't matter to you because, I don't know, you have this way of, like, not hurting . . . isn't it . . . so you don't tell each other stories any more, or sing songs together, or make things up, and practice magic, and now you're my husband and we have our baby but we're still in the bloody middle of it . . . all over again."

She stopped then, looking away.

"I know . . . ," she went on after a while, "what he said to you was, you and me, we'll change the world. That's what I said to you myself. That's the way we talk . . . all of us . . . bravado . . ."

He picked up the glass knife and inserting it into its leather sheath placed it carefully back in his briefcase.

"But you people are really very bright," he murmured finally, tucking himself back into bed beside her. "What you've managed to achieve is astonishing. That's what we need to build on. If I couldn't see that we wouldn't have got this far with it, nor would Granny Valerie Denning, or old Edward Caplin, or Uncle Horace, or any of them. It's too bloody late now, anyway."

Chapter Thirty Seven

"I'm sorry, Brigadier, but your board meeting has been cancelled. Our apology that you weren't notified, something of an emergency."

"Who says so?"

The secretary made no reply beyond handing him a large manila folder before turning on her heels and disappearing back down the corridor.

Mike stepped forward a few paces to peer through Jamieson's door.

"What's up, Peter?"

"Damned if I'd know, young Michael. Better talk to old Fergusson, if you ask me. Stuff and bloody nonsense. Spate of killings apparently. Department heads, party officials, political inner circle; assassinations. Rather ugly. Good riddance I say."

"Who?"

Not answering, Peter simply stood up from his desk and sauntered over to the wall screen and turned it on. Premier Jenkins was talking live, plainly agitated and not making a lot of sense.

"Like to do a little job for me?"

"What? Yes, of course. What have you got?'

He took the USB stick from his pocket and handed it over. "Check the log files for me, will you? I'm interested on the packet echoes and Trace Route files. See if you can find out for me who they are; where they came from."

Peter inserted the device into a spare port and quickly began to run streams of data down the big screen on the wall behind his desk. Within seconds it started to sort itself into graphs and tables, and zooming out into complex networks until nodes took form in them he pressed a few keys and superimposed a large street map of the city.

"Special Branch," he murmured finally.

"Cheeky bastards. They ought to know better. Which nodes, and whose offices?"

"Ah, yes, routing through Southern Districts most of it, trying to make out it's TRG on Landsraad security. And look, New City Police HQ, tracing back to the Premier's office."

"All right," Mike said. "Shut everything down. That's an order."

"Can't be serious! Anyway, can't. Not as easy as that; iVEX, old bean. Wide Field Array, way up there on the Tanami."

"What can you do, then?"

"You are serious. Let me see then. We haven't had a power failure in 135 years, what? Not with all the solar panels, and windmills and back-up gensets on the grid. Good thing, eh? Best part of the entire system. Firewalls are all up, 2048-bit encryption, can't get better."

Mike stood facing him, frustrated now. No doubt the man possessed undoubted genius but at times he was also a complete nutcase, and very annoying.

"Not so damned fast, eh? Hold up, Brigadier," the man muttered almost to himself. "What I can do is make it LOOK like we're all shut down, out of action. Old Vexy is tucked right away down there in the basement, and nobody aside from me knows behind what bloody door. Could be the air-conditioning. Clever, don't you think. Smart move that."

"OK now, watch what happens."

Peter deftly flicked a few switches, then poking his hands up somewhere else, up under the console somewhere, suddenly the entire room went dark. The big screen on the wall went dark and the huge lens set in his desk slowly dimmed and turned a dull grey-black, with every light on the console behind him flickering out.

"Right, then, nearly there," he chirped. Waltzing about the office he knocked over a chair or two, and scattered a few papers and old empty hamburger cartons and plastic cups about. Finally he pulled one of the smaller side panels open and left it that way, wiring bared, as if the machine had been broken into and sabotaged.

Stepping over to Mike he took a thin tablet from his pocket, and flicking his fingers across the screen brought up his Live Earth console in miniature.

"Right, then. You have a dock in your 'copter, we'll plug it in there. We can go now if you like. Just a moment."

Outside in the corridor he left the door slightly ajar, and randomly tapping a few icons on the small screen abruptly the lightest film of dust began to settle on everything inside.

Chapter Thirty Eight

Keeping the Gascoyne battalion on alert, Mike moved his two southern battalions steadily north-westerly to bivouac just south and east of the broad Gwambyrang plain, out of sight behind the broken country bordering the place. His own headquarters he established on the high western rim so he could monitor operations and keep an eye on the milling stream of humanity spilling out of the city through the escarpment on that side.

The helicopter gunship squadron he split into two flights, sending the first south to patrol the rough end of the scarp bordering the southern end of the coastal plain, to create a no-man's land down there between this lot and the protest crowd around Landsraad. Bede's mounted companies patrolled to the south of him along the eastern slopes of the scarp itself. Jitendra's men he left on bivouac behind the breakaway at the far eastern end of the wide plain, with instructions to have his men ride the boundaries, casting north if necessary, and deter any strays from wandering.

The field secure, he ordered his big transporters in to airlift huge fresh water tanks and soup kitchens with demountable pantries and vegetable bins out onto the plain, strategically in groups to focus the crowd where he wanted them to congregate, not worrying about ablutions in the time available. They would just have to piss standing up, and shit where they could, and take care of their own mess. The bright sparks among them will eventually think to dig latrine pits, no doubt.

"Excuse me, sir," one of his staffers interrupted his thoughts.

"Yes, what is it?"

"They'll need entertaining. Once they settle in they'll start to fidget."

"So, what are you thinking about?"

"Rock concert, DJs, something familiar. Once the music starts they won't move from where they are."

"How soon can you arrange it?"

"Day, at the most. It will take that long for the main crowd to arrive anyway."

"All right, go. Make it a Big Day Out. Spread the word and get some posters up around the soup kitchens."

He paused a moment, thinking, then called out, "No, wait Captain."

"Sir?"

"Those concert people, they have their own security, do they?"

"Yes, sir."

The phone was ringing and he picked it up and placed it on hold.

"Tell then to bring as many as they can. They can take the heat off us. Once they're in place issue orders for our men to pull back into the forest. Maintain boundaries only. No alcohol, no drugs, is that clear?"

"Yes, sir."

"Barker."

It was Horrie Caplin.

"We're through, Michael. I'll send the details in dispatches."

"Already?"

"Yes, we did it. Government has collapsed with all the major parties conceding the dilemma. There will be a double dissolution with a fresh election in 5-6 weeks. Parliament is prorogued until then. Jenkins will remain as caretaker. Speak to you later."

The moment he put the phone down it rang again.

"Barker."

"Quoll Squad, Sir."

"What have you?"

"Accomplished, Sir."

"Branch?"

"No longer exists, Sir."

"Escaped prisoners?"

"All dead, Sir. Their entire group are dead, prisoners and accomplices. Caught in the cross fire, I understand."

"Thank you. Out."

He set the phone down again and stood to gaze out over the hot dusty plain, the distant haze kicked up by probably 100,000 pairs of feet with 2-3 times that number due to arrive within the next day or so.

As he watched a smaller, more definite dust plume caught his eye, coming across his field of view in the clearer air about a kilometre out. He trained his scope on it.

Ajani was staring directly at him, holding his pretty horse steady as he did so, then stepped it out in front of Tempi and his friends and abruptly stood in his stirrups and saluted him.

"Lieutenant."

"Yes, sir?"

"Those mounted cadets down there, can you see them? One thousand metres at 350°. They are not supposed to be there."

"Who are they, sir?"

"Colonel Jitendra's boys, must have strayed. He'll be 20 kilometres from here. Do me a favour and go down there, will you, and escort them up here for me."

THE END

ABOUT THE AUTHOR

As an anthropologist, novelist and writer Gil Hardwick is a gifted and imaginative author. Over many years working as a field ethnographer in the vast Australian inland he has met real characters and had real-life adventures, bringing his personalities and his plots to vibrant life. Writing from life, he neither shies away from real social issues and at times confronting dilemmas.

Well worth reading.

www.ingramcontent.com/pod-product-compliance
Lightning Source LLC
Chambersburg PA
CBHW070936130626
46555CB00001B/460